THE FALLING ASTRONAUTS

THE FALLING ASTRONAUTS BARRY N. MALZBERG

AFTERWORD BY UMBERTO ROSSI

A∅P

ANTI-OEDIPUS PRESS

PRAISE FOR BARRY N. MALZBERG

"There are possibly a dozen genius writers in the genre of the imaginative, and Barry Malzberg is at least eight of them."
—Harlan Ellison

"Malzberg makes persuasively clear that the best of science fiction should be valued as literature and nothing else."
—The Washington Post

"One of the finest practitioners of science fiction."
—Harry Harrison

"Barry N. Malzberg's writing is unparalleled in its intensity and in its apocalyptic sensibility. His detractors consider him bleakly monotonous and despairing, but he is a master of black humor, and is one of the few writers to have used science fiction's vocabulary of ideas extensively as apparatus in psychological landscapes, dramatizing relationships between the human mind and its social environment in an SF theater of the absurd."
—The Encyclopedia of Science Fiction

"The writer who attempts to use the SF mythos as Malzberg has is bedevilled by the inappropriateness of the 'rules' pertaining to the production and consumption of mass-produced fiction."
—Brian Stableford

"Malzberg is a true hero."
—The Magazine of Fantasy & Science Fiction

"There is no one, with the possible exception of Philip K. Dick, whose works, each one of them, are so unpredictable or so outrageous and outraged."
—Theodore Sturgeon

"Barry Malzberg is one of science fiction's most literate and erudite writers."
—New York Times Book Review

The Falling Astronauts
Copyright © 1971 by Barry N. Malzberg
ISBN: 978-0-9905733-8-8
Library of Congress Control Number: 2016962264

First published in the United States by Ace Books

First Anti-Oedipal Paperback Edition: March 2017

www.rawdogscreaming.com

Afterword © 2017 by Umberto Rossi

Cover Design by Matthew Revert
www.matthewrevert.com

Interior Layout by D. Harlan Wilson
www.dharlanwilson.com

Anti-Oedipus Press
Grand Rapids, MI

www.anti-oedipuspress.com

ALSO BY BARRY N. MALZBERG

NOVELS

FICTION COLLECTIONS

Out from Ganymede
The Many Worlds of Barry Malzberg
Down Here in the Dream Quarter
The Best of Barry Malzberg
Malzberg at Large
The Man Who Loved the Midnight Lady
The Passage of the Light
In the Stone House
On Account of Darkness and Other SF Stories
The Very Best of Barry N. Malzberg

NONFICTION

The Engines of the Night
Breakfast in the Ruins
The Business of Science Fiction

"Get me out of here. Get me out of here!"
—Scott Carpenter

✳

For Joyce, Stephanie Jill and Erika Cornell

THE CONQUEST OF SPACE

Every day I pick up
The newspaper, and I read about my hands:

On page seven,
Here is another strangulation in Berlin.
A Picture Story from Buenos Aires
Shows animals torn apart in the field.

In Russia,
A whole crop is destroyed.
Witnesses in the Capitol
Describe what appears to be a bronze thumb,
Fifty feet high
And weighing, probably, more than thirty tons.
Which is erected
Overnight in the White House garden;
Similar eruptions occur;
In a week,
Washington is crushed,
Entire streets are twisted into little ropes.

The police are working on it.
Police everywhere are on the case.
Mondays,
I turn myself in.
They are getting tired of that.

One thing against me
Is that I have no fingerprints.
None.
I cannot leave a trace.

I would like to love my hands.
I would like to get into impossible hearts
And fix them from the inside.

But they are too big,
My hands.
And they are flying all over the world
And I cannot stop
Them.

—Trim Bissell (1967)

I

DOCKING MANEUVER: He feeds himself into her slowly, feeling the tentative hold, the slow, circling motions of orbit, anxious to grasp, but fearful that if he does so the connection will be broken . . . and the other craft will dart off into space, squeaking denial. So much, then, for inter-spatial hookups; so much for programming. *Gentle, gentle, you fool,* he cautions himself and tumbles into her fully, taking the small, winking clutch of her thighs as she eases him against her; then he falls on top of her and begins the laborious instants of gathering. Connection.

Connection. Up and down, in and out, scatology moving in the foreground against a deeper, almost solemn hush. He begins to talk to her in a high, level voice: persuasion, intimacy. "Come on," he says, "come on now, faster," hoping to wrench from her by persuasion what he cannot by insistence, and slowly, slowly she opens underneath or perhaps it is only an image of opening which seizes him. And in any event, it is too late. Mission destroyed. Control lost the linkage. We done blown a fuse out here, gentlemen, hold for further instructions. Stay in your positions. Make no false adjustments.

And so he spills into her, gasping, broken, feeling her move away from him, feeling her cycle into a new trajectory, and he does not know whether it is fulfillment or pain which causes him to topple from her so abruptly and lie beside, his eyes open to the blankness of ceiling, his chest rising so unevenly that if he had not had such a close physical check so recently, he would be doubtful of his heartbeat. He hears machinery: the tick of gears, whine of engines, clash of transmission and hiss of static in the nighttime air and from the far background he seems to hear a voice. Dedicated, low and monomaniacal, the voice is telling him that he has, after all, performed his maneuvers well.

Machinery, the voice says with terrible reason. It's all machinery. Think of yourself as an engine. Why worry about the work? Do machines worry? Alpha, beta, delta, null. You really think too much already, kid.

"Fuck you," the astronaut tells the voice, but then reconsiders, retreats. "Crazy," he says instead, but only to himself. "I'm crazy. I know that I'm crazy. Already. Please." This is less an insight than a prayer, however, and so, without speaking, he turns on his side, away from his wife, clutching the pillow as if it were space-gear, and counsels himself slowly into a dark sleep, pierced with murmurs. His wife says nothing. Perhaps she had never awakened. He knows he will have to stop this. There are limits to the woman.

Yes. Limits. If the obsession continues, he will have to talk openly with the psychiatric division, tell them the withheld parts, and he does not know if he can take this. They will understand nothing; they only want to repair him. They do not want to listen; nevertheless—if this does not stop—he will have to try. But now it is late, late at night and tired, and in the spaces of his fatigue the astronaut can only think of her, his wife, as the tumbling craft, barely linked to him in the ether, sliding toward the Moon as he holds against the fall and straddles his fear. He can not give in to this. He has higher obligations. One must. Be. Responsible.

II

He is not The Astronaut. This depersonalization must cease; he must heed the advice of the psychiatrists and keep his "name," his "identity" in front of him at all times. "The Astronaut" came later; it was only a function. *His* name is Richard Martin. "Richard Martin." In the bed he says it once, quietly.

He must hold on to this name at all times. Sometimes people call him "Dick" but he does not like this. His wife has a name too. It is Susan. Susan Martin, his wife. She is thirty-five years old and a long time ago he loved her. *Get inside*, she had muttered, the first clumsy time he had fucked her, *get inside quick*. He had never known that women before could be driven. *Inside*.

Inside, Richard Martin. In darkness, he dives and thinks that above the Moon again, he can hear the men screaming.

III

Presently, Richard Martin dreams, or thinks that he is dreaming. In this speculation, he is holding a press conference. Hundreds of newsmen from the specialized publications as well as the major outlets are before him in a large conference room; behind him sits the Public Relations Director, ready to assist if he falls into a snare but now, quiet, his hands clasped as if in meditation. The Public Relations Director seems to be thinking of something else. Possibly he despises Martin but the personal cannot enter into his kind of job. Martin has become very sensitive to reactions; he is aware of all of this.

The astronaut—Richard Martin—has not wanted to stand but one of the rules of the agency is that active personnel in the public eye must show proper poise and physical condition at all times. (Thanks largely to him now, the appropriations situation is touchier than ever and no lapses are tolerated.) He will not lose active status until his papers are processed; he is still an instrument of the agency, a colonel in fact; he will be cooperative and he will stand. Nevertheless, Martin feels as if he might collapse; it is only a neurasthenic reaction, of course, but were he to fall to the floor from a fainting weakness of the ankles, how would this be explained to the press? Or would they care? Possibly some of them have had the experience themselves, being overcome by gas at explosions or prostitutes at sex scandals.

"How does it feel?" a thin man with mad eyes asks to begin, "how do you feel to be out of the agency? Do you have any sense of loss? Do you feel somehow that your leaving under these circumstances is an admission of failure? How can you circle the Moon and not two months later say that you feel too old for space? It sounds pretty false to me. A fuller explanation if you will. The truth of this. We need it; we must enable the public to understand."

"Let me point out," Martin says, hunching his shoulders, shaking his head, trying not to look at the man directly because he knows that if he does he will be on the verge of a confrontation that he could not bear, "let me point out, as I say, this: that I feel now to be the time for me to resign active duty because my particular usefulness to this project is at an end. My place can be taken by any one of fifty or sixty qualified men, all of them capable of doing what I did with the same adequacy. There was a time in the early days of the program where each man, because of his training, might have been irreplaceable or at least very expensive, but that is no longer true. I don't really think so. This is a big operation here now and I decided that it was time for me to step out of the way and let one of the younger fellows have the chance.

"After all," he says with what he hopes to be a disarming grin, "once you've seen space once, you've seen it fifty times."

"You know something?" the mad-eyed reporter says, "you're full of shit. You're lying to us, Martin; that isn't the reason you quit at all. There's nothing that would make any of you monkeys in the program quit except fear or mental illness or threats and that's what has happened here. It's obvious. All of it. That's what happened, you just caved in mister or colonel or whatever the hell they call you and you owe it to us to lay it on the line. The nation demands! The nation must be served! We can no longer accept your public relations lies! The press is the last bastion of freedom and truth!"

"But that's not true," Martin says and notes that his voice seems to have broken. (There is precedent for that; let it not worry him unduly.) "That's simply not true; when we circled the Moon it was not fear which filled me because I knew fear well, the whole sense of it, and had conquered that a long time ago. Fear is nothing. It was the isolation. Terror at the isolation, terror at the maddening realization that all I had to do at any moment was push the button and make the escape fire, the pretty flames of flight; oh God, the cunning knowledge that I could abandon the two bastards down there and no way that they could ever be recovered and oh boy, the compulsion, the sense of imminence, it was all too much for me. Too much! You have no idea of what we live through out there, the horrors of it!" he bellows . . . and lunges toward the tormenting news freak but before he can go even two steps, the Public Relations Director has intervened, has put a hand on his shoulder, is guiding him gently toward the podium, murmuring.

"Don't listen to them," he says, "there's no reason to listen. They're only wolves and all they want is a cheap, easy headline. It isn't personal. They don't even know what's going on," the Director counsels, the Director of course being qualified on every aspect of the program . . . and the scene seems to shift, then, there is a lapse of time, nothing being quite as it was in any event and maybe it was not that way in the first place. A lady reporter with huge glasses and ascendant breasts is demanding the female view of the space program. Specifically, what does his wife think of his resignation to say nothing of the Mission? How long are women going to be excluded from the program except in the capacity of public relations wives who apparently have no passion? Was his wife the one to force him to resign? Did he defer to her wishes? Does he believe in mutual orgasms and women's rights in the bed? Does he remember having any feeling for her at all as they passed over the craters or do the men really make dirty jokes off the audio?

"Her feelings are ambivalent," Martin says carefully, pausing on the difficult word to get it out just right, *am-bi-vay-lent*. "Absolutely ambivalent you know. She's hated this program you see from the very first and everything that it stood for too and so on and so forth but then on the other hand she was pretty well kept under wraps like all of the women and she stood by for a long, long time. But while she was standing by, whatever love she had for me ended. It curdled into something harder and brighter and more desperate than love and struck me in the night . . . and all of this because I could not leave. How could I leave? The investment was enormous and besides it was the only thing I knew. Something terrible would have to happen to me to force me to go and by the time it came along there was no difference.

"We were one of the few families in the program without children, you see. That's bad; it's even easier for the bachelors than childless couples because the bachelors can duck the whole social insanity but we were part of it and yet no part of it. So she had nothing to do with the days, not really, and little in common with the other wives and all she wanted to do was to get out of the life. That was the way she put it, 'I want to get out of the life, Richard; I can't take this.' But she couldn't. How could she? And by that time, anything that we might have had was all gone to pieces until we were living with just the broken furniture of a marriage, that was her way of putting it, but we couldn't get evicted because that wasn't part of the program either. I know I'm not phrasing this too well but I want to be fair to her. Let me get to the point: we lived past hatred, you see, past everything but revulsion and fatigue and by the time I had the thing happen to me so that I could get out, it didn't matter anymore. It made no difference. What I'm trying to say is that she really doesn't care and probably she's going to leave me almost any time. I'd like to give you the women's point of view somewhat better on this but I can't, you see. I simply can't; I don't understand it. I think the problem is that women have nothing to do with this."

"That is quite interesting," says a short, vacant faced man who seems to be from the *Journalistic Sun*, "and we appreciate that information but you're really rambling quite a bit, colonel, and you've managed to stray away completely from the basic point of the matter. Let's stick to business if we can. Why did you want to desert those men? What would that have accomplished? Do you think your mental state was unbalanced at that time or was it something that the conditions could have done to anyone at all if they were in your position? Give me a straight answer, please. We've been following this program for almost two decades and if you gave one it would set a precedent."

"No," Martin says, "no, no, I didn't want to desert them. I didn't *want* to, I mean, it was just the perversity of the *thought* that drove me mad, you see. That I would even think such a thing, after all the training and so on; they never even gave you an indication that this kind of thing might happen to you if you got out there alone in the control capsule—"

"Oh come on," the reporter says, "we don't have the time anymore. Time is running too short on all of us now and besides, friend, we're private industry. We have to justify our time to get ourselves fired. Now listen to me: you wanted to do it, you wanted to desert them and you would have done it if you hadn't lacked the guts. You're crazy, do you know that, space monkey? You're crazy, man. They would put you into an insane asylum and take out your frontal lobes except that the press would kill the program, they'd feed all that stuff out and the craziness would kill everything, now astronauts going crazy and trying to desert, they would say, and so much for the space program. This is a nice easy cover instead. Isn't that true, rover boy? They're going to pension you out nice and slow and you might even get a desk job after this but you listen to me you twitching son of a bitch, there is absolutely no hope for you because you wanted—"

"I didn't!" the astronaut cries, "I didn't!" and lunges toward the newspaperman . . . but once again his charge is broken by the Public Relations Director, whose grasp this time is much firmer and he is saying, "That is it, that's it, this press conference is over, it is now over I tell you," while the reporters run in various directions, some toward the exits and some toward the astronaut and he feels that they are about to overwhelm him. He does not know precisely what he will be able to do in order to protect himself but as he feels the impact of the bodies pressing against him, he suspects that it may be something violent. A dark anger tears through him and he flings an arm, mutters something, coils his body for what could only be an attack but at the last instant, right before disaster, that is, the Director seizes him by an elbow and says, "Come on, come on now, just forget it; they're doing a job like anyone else and anyway there isn't a word of truth in it because you loved those men and wouldn't have hurt them for anything in the world. We know it. We know it."

Martin turns toward the Director to see if there is irony in his face but as he does so, the face changes and becomes the slick pan of the computer feeding out the tapes to him, the fucking—

IV

—Tapes that tell him exactly what to do and where to go, put them in the controls and let them guide the ship, who needs them anymore? and he cannot take this. Cannot take it. He finds that he is on the ship again and the face has become the computer and information is now battering him: an overload of information about courses and trajectories and fuel consumption and so on. Back to the damned ship again! He thought that was all behind him forever and as he turns from the computer in horror he sees that his companions are there. They are lying weightless, drifting in space, their eyes winking and he hates them. Oh, how he hates them! Now for the first time he feels that he can tell them so but as he holds his mouth ready to shout threats they begin to laugh. They laugh at him madly because they will be the ones to explore the Moon while he, the inadequate Richard Martin, will remain on the ship and this laughter destroys him. It absolutely rips him to shreds and he feels himself imploding, falling to pieces on the ship, the dim throb of the support systems unable to separate his flesh from the stink, oh God, there is so much space but there is too little space: how will he ever get away from them? How?

He waits for the scene to change again, knowing now that all of this is a dream (because nothing so terrible could be other than a dream, it would be unfair), waits there for the next assault, but as he lies suspended, gray in jelly, he comes to understand that the scene will not shift this time, it may never shift again; he is going to be in this condition forever and now it is all too much for him. He too has his limits. He tries to shriek but cannot shriek, it seems that there are ropes and the ropes are binding. He cuts his flesh against them trying to move but the voices will not let him stir and behind the voices whines and giggles and behind that the wrenching tumble of the wretched ship taking him deeper and deeper into space and beyond all that is something else still, nothing at an end, forever all of this, and he rises to peripety, vaulting toward an insight deeper than any he has known before and then—

V

—Coming against the Moon, deep in a voyage, Martin had thought that it was beautiful, and the beauty was of a sort he had never suspected before. Rather than voyaging out, the Moon had given him the feeling that he was coming in, moving into something as familiar as it was accessible, and he had hovered on the window long beyond necessity just to look at it: the faint scattering of colors at the edges, the crevices in the center that looked so deep he could hurl himself and fall forever. Into the pit of memory.

By that time he was oblivious of the two men in the ship with him. The desultory conversations of the early voyage were no more. Later on, much later, they would tell him that this was nothing for him to think about; he had been deep into what was called technically a dissociative reaction and this was normal; the forgetfulness that is, was to be expected. Just stay cool and swing with the treatment . . . but just as the nurses in the hospital had frightened him with their aseptic stares, so the men in the ship had scared him for other reasons: the occasional jarring encounters, the huddle of forms, the constant banging and scuffle of bodies which had to do with the logistics of adjustments. He had nothing in common with them. It was impossible to take them seriously. During the two telecasts they had managed a forced and extended joviality, a sense of friendship which he hoped was impressing watchers through the machinery, but between the broadcasts he had had nothing to do with these others and they, possibly, nothing to do with him.

(It was hard to recall. He seemed to recollect that now and then they would exchange jokes. The jokes were always scatological and centered mostly around anal functioning, which was strange. How, once you have been in a spacecraft, could anal functioning ever be funny again? Also, they had talked of buggering one another, made plans to do it during the broadcasts, just to liven up the format, but he had a horror of homosexuality for reasons which went beyond the ship and once he had threatened to kill if he were touched.)

He did not hate these men—and this was something to hold on to, he had to believe that he did not hate them, he had had their interests, finally, at heart—it was nothing like that at all. It was simply that he could not bear their presence because their being in such close quarters in the craft kept him from thinking.

It was important that he think. Now, more than ever, he had to take things seriously, pass them on in review, make deductions. Looking at the Moon, he knew that he had to get his life into perspective, get a lock on it, decide what he had made of himself and what he would do with the remainder of his years. He was thirty-seven years old; it was time to take stock. But there was no time, damn it: never any time at all. There were the telecasts and the transmissions and check-outs and dry runs and discussions and always (except during the telecasts and sleep) a constant rattle of insane orders, busywork, complaints from Control which had good reason to be nervous because the appropriations were in big trouble and they did not want to blow this mission too. In the sleep periods, which were the only time when they would shut up, he was still not able to do his thinking because of all the breathing and cries, muttering and belching, in the craft. So on that basis alone, if he had been a hating man, he could have hated the other two. But he wasn't. He didn't. He knew that. And even if he did, it would never have been personal. It was the best that he wished them. In the abstract.

He was not a hating man. He would never have gotten through half the tests if he had been. He was, in fact, a terribly reasonable man in a tough situation and that was why the business of abandoning the men had jarred him so much. He was not used to thoughts like these and nothing in his experience had equipped him to deal properly with them. The realization that he could void the mission (and very spectacularly in the bargain) had hit him cross-angles, almost offhandedly, somewhere midway and since that realization the rest of the trip had been hell . . . hell alternating with glimpses of and thoughts about the Moon. (The Moon was a neutral; he had no feelings about it one way or the other.) The two others had meant so little to him, the focus of the voyage had been so entirely shifted away from him, that in the thirty-six hours that they were gone, when he had lived in the control capsule, circling in dilatory orbit, he had had to put away the compulsion almost by the minute. There had not been an uninterrupted interval of even seconds during which he did not think about what he would like to do to them.

It would be so easy, so easy to abandon, but hearing on the inside revolution the cackle and peep of their voices, he knew that it would not be so easy. It would, in fact, be damned hard; there were all those consequences to think about and so he had relied upon the saner, more fully-trained part of him to pull him through. In the empty capsule he had prayed against the porthole:

oh God, let me not leave them, they are so helpless now, please grant me this, that I will not leave them, and I promise you that when I return I will quit this program and never have any part of it again . . . only grant me re-mission, let me stay

The sound of their voices would bleat in the void, the high-pierced babble of their terror, the knowledge of an abandonment so final it was incomprehensible, sinking in further and further—

Voyage in. Voyage out.

Richard Martin staggers from the bed. His wife lies in pale, lumpish sleep beside him. He begins to dress for the day. Processing on his shift to press liaison officer for the next mission will not be completed for several days yet and in the bargain—oh boy—there will be another press conference today.

He thinks he hears her call his name in sleep but does not turn.

This was June.

VI

Cometh September.

Richard Martin, Lieutenant Colonel (ret'd), USAF, faces the press yet again in his capacity as information officer for the new mission. His eyes are clear, a certain blankness around the cheekbones signaling perhaps nothing more than the effect of severe discipline. His posture and gestures are well within normal military limits as positively defined. A cigarette is inserted neatly between his index and second fingers, the decision having been for a mild smoking-relaxant some time ago. (You can live perfectly normally, they had assured him. You've had something of a breakdown under stress but it is all explicable and we can be sure that if the stress does not recur, the problem will not either. Do not pamper yourself. Do not be concerned. And remember at all times that no one except yourself truly knows what happened; you are not on display. You can have a long, rich, satisfying life if only you accept the fact that you have limits and having touched them once, know you will never have to touch them again. It could have happened to anyone at all.)

The cigarette burns his fingers and he readjusts it to a new angle, an inexperienced smoker. "Everything is on schedule," he tells the press. "The releases which you have taken will fill you in more completely than I could on the schedule of the voyage, its intended objectives and so on. Everything is go-normal at the present time and the countdown continues. Are there any questions at this time?"

"When will we meet the men?" asks a lady member. "We can expect a conference before launch, can't we? We were definitely promised."

"I suppose so," says Richard Martin. "Plans in that regard have not, however, been yet finalized. The primary thing is for the countdown and checkout; as you must understand, any contacts with the press must be fitted around that basic obligation."

"How do things look?" someone wants to know. "You say everything is on schedule but are there any qualifying factors? Or not? I'm sorry."

Unlike the reporters in his dream, the members of the press whom Martin has met so far are docile, cooperative, amenable. Only a certain smugness to their bearing, a scent of history in their winks indicate that they may have private thoughts on the matter. "Everything is great," he says. "Just great. No qualifying factors whatsoever."

("The thing you will understand," the press chieftain has told him, "is that they've been through it so often and have been so tied in with the agency, most of them, for so long, that it isn't even a question of inquiry anymore. First off, it's a media business; television and pickup, the press is increasingly marginal. Secondly, it all has to do with cooperation. More than anything else, and let me tell you this, you find that they're writing direct from our releases. This may not be the best way to break you in but on the other hand," the chief added, "on the other hand, you're here for reasons which have very little to do with media, Dick, and I want you to relax. You'll find things going very easy here. If you understand how things work you'll be inclined to do your job that much better; you'll find them a very eager and cooperative bunch if you just don't push them too hard and try to depend on their reaction.

("I did a little work like this at the academy," Martin had said pointlessly, "of course, I guess that that isn't the kind of preparation you're thinking of," and the chief had laughed and said that no, that wasn't exactly what he would have in mind for a real press aide, although he didn't expect that Martin would fuck him up at all. It had been a jovial, if brief meeting; only later on had Martin, thinking it over, begun to understand that the joviality was working on something more profound. The chief was afraid of him. Almost everyone in the project, even the medical staff, was a little fearful but in the case of the chief it had been more direct and personal; he did not know if Martin would be able to hold himself together in public but in the chief's case the disassembly would be particularly damaging. He had a nice easy job, the chief; he did not want problems at this point and Martin was unpredictable. Martin had resolved to stay with this line of thought, possibly seek out the chief socially so that he could prove himself to be a rational, organized man with only a little, as the psychiatrists had said, stress trouble, but his superior had become less accessible all the time; now it was a job, obviously, that he was supposed to work out through memo.)

"Everything looks all right," Martin says again. There is a pause; generalities have never been his strong point. "On schedule, as I say. No interruptions. Good engineering support."

"How is the Busbys' daughter?"

"Oh," Martin says. Katherine "Kit" Busby, the only daughter of the crew's youngest member, Colonel John Busby, has been hospitalized for a broken leg and there was some doubt, a few days ago, that Busby would be able to give full concentration to the mission, even some talk that he might, in deference to his concern, be replaced at the last moment. But the girl has been making good progress in the hospital (a special line has been set up between the girl's room and Busby's quarters so that they can talk during his off-duty hours) and the question now seems to be whether Katherine will be well enough, two days hence, to be transported to the launch site. "She's doing very well," he says. "Apparently she has a motorized wheelchair and has been all over the hospital, telling everyone about her father. The staff is crazy about her and are planning to have a special party on launch day if she can't be at the site itself. All in all, it's been an exciting experience for her; under the circumstances she may be better off in the hospital than outside, being attended. And of course the hospital is pretty happy about it too."

That seems to cover it. There is an uneasy silence, however, during which he feels that somehow he might have missed a vital point of information. He digs through the papers on the clipboard until he finds the page with notes on Katherine "Kit" Busby to see if there is anything he can add. Twelve years old. Only child. Father a widower but no need to get into that one now. Sixth grade in private school, possibly a little bit slow for her age, although isn't the sixth grade exactly where twelve years old is supposed to be? He cannot remember. Strange. Calls her father "the colonel" and plays clarinet in the school band. Marching band? No discrimination seems to have been made on this.

The pause continues, attenuates. Martin understands that the press is suffering no less than he; the majority of these reporters have been assigned from the syndicates or as extras from their newspapers. The regulars do not go to these conferences but pick it up later off the wire and write feature stories. Most of the reporters in this room, then, accept the fact that their being there marks them as second-stringers. This has not always been true—press conferences, he remembers, were very big once—but the project is no longer a choice assignment. There have been too many flights, too many complications, and too much going on elsewhere to allow any reporter assigned a launch to feel that he is in the front lines of developing events. Martin can appreciate this. The press, these reporters, thirty or forty of them clumped uneasily in the center of the room, eyeing him at the lectern, would rather be somewhere else and no amount of conferences, releases or discussions can do more than nail that insight into them. "Captain Allen is feeling much better as well," he volunteers. "The cold symptoms seem to have disappeared. It now appears, as you'll note in the release, that the symptoms were symptomatic. I mean psychosomatic. Excuse me, I got those two terms mixed up."

"Psychosomatic?" a tall fellow with a camera draped around his neck asks blandly. "Are you suggesting to us, sir, that the commander of this mission, a ten-year veteran of the program, a veteran of three prior missions no less, would be having himself an attack of nerves?"

"Nothing of the sort," Martin says quickly. "You misunderstand the context. Under the conditions of heavy training, certain symptoms may spontaneously appear and disappear without any relation to illness. I can recall from my own experience this sort of thing happening. It doesn't mean that you're sick."

"Well, sir, I don't mean to interrupt you but there seems to be something of a story here if we could just stay on this point for a second. Are you saying that the Commander is imagining symptoms? Or is the implication—"

"He has no symptoms anymore. I said that there had been a complete remission."

"No, you didn't quite say that at all. You just mentioned that now."

"It's the same thing."

"Is it? Because if he had been having symptoms which your doctors think are all in his head, that would say interesting things, wouldn't it, about the man? Like an attack of nerves, which I suggested. Of course, it doesn't have to be nerves, it could be something else. I think that we're entitled to a little more discussion here."

"There is no problem," Martin says. "I can tell you from my own experience that this kind of thing will happen often in the final preparations and means nothing. It has nothing to do with nerves; it's purely somatic. Commander Allen is an experienced man, surely one of the most experienced in the program, or he would never have been selected for this important position."

"Well, sir, not to be impolite, but what if I wrote a story and in this story I said that the commander of this particular flight was showing a little hypochondria? Would that be a fair lead? You see, I haven't been covering this stuff for years like most of the people in this room. I'm just a simple guy off the county political desk and what I'd like to do is to try to get a fresh perspective here. Now if you want to evade the question that's fine. You just say right here that you have no comment and we'll let this thing drop."

"I'm not being evasive," Martin says and then realizes that his tone has become strident: precisely what the hell is happening in this conference? And what does he think he is doing?

"Now you just listen to me," he says more quietly. "There is no basis here whatsoever—"

"He's baiting you, Colonel," a reporter says from the front row. "He's just trying to get a rise out of you for no particular reason."

"I'll handle this."

"No need for you to," the reporter says cheerfully and stands. "Now cut it out, Perkins," he says to the camera-holder. "This is a routine press briefing and everything is very much in order. Leave this man alone. I'm experienced," the reporter says, giving Martin an almost confidential wink. "Most of us have been through this any number of times, and believe me, you have absolutely no cause for concern. You're doing beautifully. Perkins is playing games; he has to amuse himself in some way. I enjoy correcting people. You see, Colonel, everything is a relative phenomenon after all."

"But I'm not playing games," Perkins says. "I'm trying to get at the truth. The trouble with this agency is that it's never held the truth to be too much of an object; the aim is public relations. But behind public relations, my publication believes, there is apt to be more than a little truth somewhere and I'm being paid to get at it. Now most of your reporters, sir, are more part of the staff than part of their newspapers, so when a man comes in here with a little legitimate curiosity—"

"Let the man be," the short reporter says authoritatively. "You don't really know what the hell is going on here."

"I can handle this," Martin says. He lifts his hands to say something compelling, something central and forceful which will utterly demolish this man and leave him without the threat of further maddening inquiry, but something happens to him in the middle of this gesture. He realizes that he has nothing to say and that he cannot deal with the press at this moment because he has lost the capacity to say something ordered and reasonable which will channel and cancel inquiry.

"I guess that is it then," he says vaguely and leaves the room. He seems to move in a dense, private patch of air; the reporters watch him go quietly. A few shout that they still have questions, clarifying queries, materials to pick up but they are silenced by the others or at least what they say is allowed to drift off without urgency. By this stage of the proceedings they should be getting used to them; Martin has sieges of vagueness during which he cannot account for his behavior but feels he must withdraw.

He finds himself standing outside the door of the press room, the reporters still clumped within, and an impulse seizes and shakes him: he wants to peek inside and announce that they are all recruited for the Moon voyage, every last one of them; they will remain under tight security until further notice and will then occupy expanded quarters in his mind . . . but he restrains himself, acknowledging that gestures of this sort will only complicate the serious public relations problem of the agency, and instead he walks quickly down the hall, forcing determination into his stride, the clipboard hard in his hand, feeling like one of the goddamned levers which he would have to push to break pressure at the time that there was a buildup in the capsule. The capsule always seemed to be expanding, small deadly hisses of air opening his eyes in sleep, moving through the craft like a bad conscience unsealed.

Ah, I don't know what's wrong with me, Martin murmurs, and a vision of Commander Allen comes to him. Commander Allen has a cold; Commander Allen is out there in space with a bad cold; Commander Allen sits in his bathrobe before the controls wheezing with ague, raising a handkerchief weakly to his sputtering mouth as he mumbles instructions to the crew, watching the Moon come up bright and deadly against them. *Give me my tea, men*, Allen murmurs, and the image winks out.

VII

The three men on the mission are named Joseph Busby, William Davis, and the Commander, Roger Allen. He does not know any of them well at all: this group was in an entirely different cycle of the program, recruited far later, and always in a different stage of training. It is difficult to maintain contact with most of the astronaut-staff; this might have been possible in the earlier days of the project but now it is simply too large. Everyone has his own interests.

He recalls that Davis's wife once made a filthy remark about him to his own wife while drunk at a party; he knows that Allen, who was on one of the first orbitals, is supposed to have prevented a man on a line from panicking in space and had talked him back to the ship without interference from the ground. He knows that Busby lost his wife under strange and tragic circumstances. But all of this, even the filthy remark, are just pieces of information, slots of data which produce no sense of connection. It is hard to have any personal feelings about this crew and in addition they have been locked into their closed cycle for several months now, readying for this flight.

The point of the training, of course, is to produce the closest concentration and interaction among the members of a crew; they must dwell so totally among themselves once the serious training begins, that only the back-ups really have anything in common. This part of it is perfectly all right with Martin; one of the things that the Accident has done for him is to give him a total disinclination to become involved with astronauts. (Or anyone else, come to think of it.) If he never speaks to anyone manning the ships again, he will be perfectly content. He has nothing to say. That business is all over.

On the other hand, this cannot quite be managed. They live in segregated housing, in clearly defined astronauts' "sections" in the town for one thing, and for another the only socialization really possible is with others on the project. Even now he must go to some parties. He has been fortunate in certain ways: his wife's increasing hatred and dissociation has undercut their popularity and there are many invitations they no longer receive. In addition to that, a certain real hostility which she has built up in her direction over these years has managed to keep their contacts limited. (He guesses that there is some hostility coming his way as well but that is a different issue; also the medical staff had promised that no one knew of his difficulties but they . . . and the secret was safe; it had been blocked from ground transmission at the onset of the trouble.)

Still, there are certain necessities. They cannot stay away from *all* the parties and it is impossible, even after his discharge, for him to move through the project without contact. He is the press officer for the new launch and this involves certain obligations. Then too, he has the ominous feeling that he could not leave now even if he wanted and that had he put it to them squarely and demanded that he be permitted to quit the project, a hand would have touched him with cunning, a voice would have said, "Can't have none of that right now, Martin, you *are* to stay in this project at the present time," the voice hitting the accent on the preposition in the old military way, fingers squeezing his arm and Martin, in a flurry of salutes and sweat, would have had to quit the office in a good deal more disgrace than the way he had when he let them handle it.

At least he is the press officer and they have given him a fair salary—they have put him at the GS-17 level, probationary status, more money than he has ever made in his life; it is a strange thing how little he thought of money until recently—and they cannot take away from him the pride that he has somehow managed the job. Nor can they take away the promise; he knows that the promise is secure. The medical staff would not lie to him and the knowledge of his disaster on the flight is lodged only with them and with him. Even the other two have no clear idea of exactly what happened in the capsule during the time that they were on the Moon. (He has not seen them since the landing; he understands that they have left the base.) Even his wife is not sure what happened although in her case it is somewhat different; she sleeps beside him and he knows that he is talking, talking a great deal during the night. And she can make her own connections. But he will not discuss it with her. Only later. Some other time. When this is all behind them.

Possibly in a few months, when things are more settled and he can leave the project quietly (for being press officer is a very temporary phase, he knows; it is the job from which his exit will make no fuss at all whereas astronauts would cause interviews). The divorce action can begin and that will be time sufficient to go into all of it. He will disclose his behavior to her at that time so that she will have grounds for easy suit. But the divorce, along with the resignation, will have to wait.

He knows Davis slightly. Their backgrounds are roughly similar and so are their ages although Davis entered the program much later and from a different direction. Martin had come in from the Air Force where most of them still, in those days, were coming from; Davis, on the other hand, had been a civilian, a sociologist as a matter of fact, who was in the first substantial group of civilians recruited as a gesture to the university faction at the project who were objecting to the military overall.

Davis back then had been a big, solemn, rather stupid-looking man who had come out of the South to get a vague athletic reputation in California; after that he had done some teaching and research although Martin suspected that he wasn't that hot a sociologist. Who went into that kind of field anyway? There was no future in it. He had told Martin at the party held for the new men (these were the kind of parties you couldn't duck) that he had had some very striking ideas about the development of the socialization process which training would show as a microcosm and he hoped to be able to convert them to some professional use if only the project would enable him to keep on publishing.

Whether or not he had published during his time in service, Davis had accepted a commission quietly a few months later when there was a revolution in one of the Latin countries and sentiment began to drift, for a change, back toward the military. He had even gone into an intensive training cycle preparing him to be the first sociologist in space. That was important to him, he had said, that someone in the behavioral sciences would have the same opportunity given test pilots and men in the hard sciences, and Martin guessed that he had been gratified to finally get into orbit around the Moon even though the mission had almost been a last-second abort due to scheduling difficulties and even though Davis, of all people, had used the broadcasts to come across in peculiarly saccharine fashion, wishing his wife and baby girl all the very best from the loneliest reaches of space. Hell, he had had some experience now; the second time out he would do better. Maybe he had even completed his studies on the socialization process and could take some genuine interest in the goings-on on the Moon.

Martin would have, at the point of the broadcast, appreciated the opportunity to sit and talk some with Davis: see what had happened to him after eighteen months in the program to make him turn out that way; but they were in different cycles and there was no possibility. Probably it was the heat in the capsule which due to minor dysfunction had reached a hundred and twenty degrees during certain stages of that mission.

Considering what had happened later on it had been for the best, anyway, not trying to learn from Davis. His wife, a large, constrained woman with a continuing pregnant slouch and poorly-dyed hair, had become disgracefully drunk and at one point or another had landed off in a corner with Susan where she had proceeded to analyze sexually all of the men in the room. Exactly what she had said about Martin had never been quite determined (Susan would say only that it was a disgusting accusation without any basis in fact but had refused, always, to say anything else) but deep in discussion with a physicist or somebody, Martin had been interrupted by the sound of slapping and shrieks from the corner and had seen his wife in the act of punching Alice Davis in the ribs. He had moved over quickly, done everything possible to calm her and get her out of the party—if there was one thing that they would never tolerate, it was scandal of this sort—but it had been very difficult. Susan had been crying and screaming in with the sobs and even when he got her outside and back to their home she had been unable to stop.

"We should have gotten out," she had said. "I told you years ago we should have gotten out of this thing. I can't stand it anymore . . . and now it's too late. Do you hear me? It's too late; we don't even know who we are anymore. They did that to us, they did it good."

It had been impossible to say anything to this. He had no idea of what had gone on, after all, and he knew that the incident, in terms of the way they had lived then, would never be again discussed. Somewhere he might have made a note to himself to discuss it with Davis someday, even to go to Alice Davis and try to find out what had happened, but he never quite got around to it and since they and the Davises never crossed paths again, there had been little to keep it in the front of his mind. Nothing seemed to stay in his mind anyway, except the docking procedures and computer readouts.

"I hate them," his wife said, "I hate everything about these people here. Their assurance, their smugness, their terror and underneath all of that, their cowardice . . . but I have this feeling, this *feeling*, that we're just like the rest of them and they say the same thing about us and we've got nowhere to go, we're all bottled up here and what it means is that it's always going to be this way."

It had been an odd way to look at a group of people, a significant number of whom might someday go to the Moon, but he had let it pass. In those days he had been letting most of what Susan said pass that way; the important thing was to maintain some sort of equivocal balance in the relationship so that he would be able to concentrate on his work. Much later he had started listening or at least thinking that he should listen . . . but by that time Susan was on another level and had nothing to say. They never intersected. There was no union of causes. But at least for a while they had kept talking, which under the circumstances might have been unusual.

Think of love, she had said to him in the beginning, *think of meaning, think of happiness, think of children playing in the fields.* Love, move, but as he moved inside her he could not see her face; propped over his shoulder the face turned toward the wall and once, when in a spasm, he shook her free he looked at her when she was coming and the face was full of small ropes, knotting below the surface.

Allen, on the other hand, he thinks he almost knows, although here too there has been contact of only the most fragmentary kind. There is a suggestion of connection here; in different circumstances, he might have dealt with this man.

(Is it possible that at the beginning there were only seven of these people and that they were involved in every aspect of each other's lives? What would it have been like to have been one of them? Aside from the permissions and the book rights and the commodities deals in those fruitful days with their mere seven-way split, aside from that, how did it feel? Did they care for one another at the time, could they bear to be in the same room? Or had the quality of life, as rumored, been entirely different back then?)

It was Allen who was the frenzied man at the end of the rope in space years ago, the astronaut who turned a routine spacewalk into an enormous problem because somewhere, midway, he had lost sight of the ship and panicked.

"My God, I'm blind, I can't see anything!" Allen had screamed in space and the sound, tinny through the transmission, had afflicted Martin and all the others who were listening because Allen was talking to the part in themselves they had always suspected. "I'm going crazy, I'm going blind!" Allen had shouted, "you sons of bitches, I can't stand this anymore!" but the center had alertly cut the transmission, already anticipating while Allen had screamed, "Get me back to that fucking ship! Oh mother, get me out of this! There's nothing out here at all!" and lovingly, patiently, Allen's then-commander had talked him back along the line of rope; foot by foot Allen had hauled himself in and had landed in the dock in a grateful, stammering heap. He had been the fourth or maybe the fifth man to show serious panic in space and all the more to his credit then that he has emerged, only a few years later, as the commander of his own expedition.

Naturally there has been intensive training in the interval and psychiatric purges as well. It is very doubtful that the psychiatrists would let out into space any man who gave prior indication of collapse . . . but still it is interesting that he has been named the Commander and not Davis who, despite the sociology, has as much service and more creditable background in space. Davis would never have let the sociology get in the way. Still, Allen is the Commander and Martin has heard rumors that this was not strictly an agency decision and that members of the present political party in power had maneuvered this so that eventually Allen could return to his home state and take an important Senate seat from the hands of the opposition. This is the kind of rumor which circulates more and more around the project now but it is always difficult to assess; the government would certainly lose more by putting the wrong man at the head than disposing of a difficult Senator. But then too, maybe the government simply considers all of them interchangeable.

True enough, Allen is strikingly handsome at least in repose, and his wife, Joan Johnson Allen, may be the most attractive and vivacious of all the younger wives on the project. This alone cannot totally dissolve a disaster in space. Martin suspects that most of the rumors are conjectural. Allen had had a normal reaction for a man suspended at the end of a rope turned from the ship and since then, like everyone else, he has no doubt come a long way. There is no indication of possible difficulty; of the three he is the most reserved—one might even say stuporous—and his comments have been the most contained. He looks upon this particular expedition as strictly a scientific mission, routine exploration. The agency, he feels, is in a period where it must deglamorize its business and substitute public respect and acceptance for cheap melodramatics and the hint of disaster. The key to the long-range effectiveness of the project, Allen feels, will be its scientific usefulness and it is important that it be understood in that light. This mission is a flight of three scientists to a particular site for study. The instrumentation of the ship is, by this time, foolproof; there is no point in looking for dramatics because the equipment makes a Moon expedition slightly less hazardous than visiting the home bathroom. In the long run it will be the contribution to knowledge, then, that will justify the agency and not pyrotechnics. Pyrotechnics got us a little bit of the way; now it is time for other methods.

All of these statements are printed very neatly on the press materials which Martin carries and he agrees with every word of them, even though the reporters do not want these releases. The trouble is that Allen once panicked in space and no matter how he tries to disregard this, Martin still thinks of it. The removal of the figment of danger may be the only way in which Allen feels he can meet his responsibilities and this is understandable. He could, however, be a little less pompous about it. Martin wonders if he is taking all of this a shade too personally.

He has spoken to Allen only once and then when he was introduced to him two weeks ago in his new capacity. Allen looked at him levelly and shook hands and suggested that they have a drink in his room and Martin was happy to go along with the suggestion. He still felt very strained in situations of encounter and getting into a small enclosed space for a drink, under whatever circumstances, seemed to be an advantage.

Allen and his crew had already by then been segregated into the tiny, individual quarters on the base which they would occupy up until the escort to the ship, and behind the locked door (on which a picture of a small cherub saying "God Bless Our Home" while lying sexually athwart a lamb had been cutely placed) Martin found Allen's quarters quite messy, almost disreputable, with three or four unopened bottles of scotch scattered through some dirty laundry, and with Allen giving him an enormous wink when passing that and saying it was literally the only way to deal with the goddamned system, you had to de-systematize it.

"I hear you had a little trouble out there," Allen said quite casually, while he poured the drinks, taking his down quite rapidly with the absent gulp of the expert drinker who had too many things on his mind to come to terms with the stuff. "Did you?"

"A shade. Maybe a shade."

"Don't want to talk about it? That's okay too. I wouldn't worry about it, though."

"It wasn't much," Martin said. "A little problem here or there but nothing really serious. You know." He waved an arm vaguely. "Space. Just too much damned space."

"Oh, you don't have to talk about it," Allen said, grunting, wiping his mouth with the back of a hand and prowling his fingers through an agglutination of pink undershirts lying near the bed. "I understand perfectly, I really do, and besides they probably gave you orders not to talk. Telling you it was for mental health but they mean for the cover-up. They still work the same way."

"How could it change?"

"Anyway, I just wanted to say that I had a few problems out there myself a few years ago as you may know and it doesn't mean a thing. I worked right out of it. Right away. No recurrence, nothing, and now I'm commanding a ship. So if you're worried you shouldn't be. Wanted to tell you that."

"Nice of you."

"Don't worry."

"I'm not."

"Well that's good," Allen said vaguely. "I mean, that's fine. Why should you worry? You're on your way out for one thing, you lucky bastard, and that's great. So the less we talk about it, then, the better."

"Whatever you say. Whatever you say."

"This whole thing's a piece of cake anyway, this baby here. I'm afraid it's more for Davis and the other guy than me. I'm just along for the ride, to make a senior. This will probably be the last one for me, Martin."

"Oh?"

"I could stay around a little longer. They might even squeeze another trip out of me, but there's no point to it. I'm getting tired. All of the clout is going into the younger guys in the first place and in the second, I think that they're going for a higher turnover now. I have a theory about that."

"Do you?" Martin said and raised the bottle, poured another drink. He looked with fascination as Allen began to disassemble an undershirt, tearing it into small strips which he then began, absently, to knot around the bedposts. "What's your theory? If you want to tell me."

"It's purposeful," Allen said, knotting busily. "They don't want anybody in here with more than five years seniority. Maybe they figure that after you hang around much longer than that you'd get your eyes into a lot of things. Ah, the hell with that," Allen said, finishing off a knot with a flourish, "that's all in confidence you understand. I wouldn't want that to get around."

"Yeah," said Martin, feeling vaguely discomfited, out of place, managing to stand while balancing the scotch he had not tasted. "Sure."

"You think I got something there?"

"Sure. Well, maybe. It makes sense to me."

"You're a senior man. Still. You tell me if I got a point."

"I never looked at it that way. But now that you say it, it makes sense, sure."

"I'm glad to hear you say that," Allen said, beginning now to untie a knot. "It makes me feel much better to get some confirmation. The thing is that you really can't find anyone around here you'd want to talk to."

"Don't worry about it," Martin said. "That's out of the picture. I'm just dealing with the press now; you understand that I'm not really part of the program anyway."

"But that's what I mean," Allen said harshly, standing with him, a certain light in his eyes. "You're working with the press now. The civilians. And you can talk to them as a civilian. You've got to get the truth out. The truth, do you follow me?" He took off the last strip of undershirt, chucked it back on the floor and kicked it away. "Tell them what it's like," he said. "Don't let it all be public relations, forever."

"Tell them what?"

"How it *is*, Martin. How it feels to be inside here, looking out on it."

Allen bent, took the bottle, poured himself another drink and passed it off in an uneasy swoop. "Because somebody should tell the truth. Just once. Somebody should really get a look into the way this thing works, because it just isn't all machinery, you know. There's got to be a guy inside all of this stuff, making it *work.*"

"Okay."

"Think of the guys who make it work, Martin," Allen said and put a hand on his shoulders. "I'm sorry," he said. "I guess I'm just a little keyed up by the training; you know. Five hours sleep and a lot of stimulants. I'm probably a bit edgy. Forget it. I didn't mean to get started."

"I know it isn't easy," Martin said. "I've been there, re-member?"

"Have you?"

"All the time. All the time."

"That's right, kid," Allen said and they exchanged a look, a short, open look between them and then Martin was stumbling toward the door, the glass still in his hand, nothing to be said. "But we can't tell them that, can we, Commander?"

"I'm not a Commander," Martin said, "I'm a light colonel."

"You're not a light colonel. You're a civilian."

"You're a future civilian."

"Indeed," said Allen and that was funny or at least it seemed funny at the time; oh how they laughed! Martin left Allen's quarters quickly, trying not to think about any of this too much. The man, underwear and all, might have been acting in a manner slightly unsuitable for imminent space flight. Then again, maybe he had not. In any case, what the hell was the point of dwelling on it . . . and who was he of all people to make judgments on instability? The agency was wise; it had its reasons. Perhaps Allen was merely acting, trying to draw *him* out so that he could report back to the medical staff. That would have been logical.

Still, this did not prevent him, that night or the night after, from saying to his wife that Allen might be a bit of a problem, and when Susan did not respond to this he repeated it more loudly. She said that she had heard him the first time but she was not going to talk about anything to do with the project anymore, not then, not ever, and if he had to talk about it he would have to pick up some acquaintances outside.

"I just wanted to say something, goddamnit!" he shouted. "Don't you listen to me anymore? Doesn't anything I say matter to you?"

"Only when I want it to and never if I don't, Richard."

"Well it does now. I said something to you and damn it, I want to hear—"

"Oh, Dick," she said and walked over, put her palm on his cheek in a caressing and pitying gesture which was somehow the most terrible thing she had ever done to him, "Dick, don't you understand? It's too late for any of this now. I'm not interested anymore. I don't want to hear about your Captain Allen and I don't want to hear about your job. All I want to do is to be left alone—"

"I'll leave you alone. You want to be left alone, I'll *do* it! Because I can't live this way anymore. Do you understand me?"

"Dick," she said and ran her hand down his cheek, past the neck, across the shoulder blades and finally in a flat gesture against the belly, holding him together that way. "Dick, there's no time to talk about this now. Maybe in a couple of months we can. Right now I think we should just try to do our best and go along from day to day, see you get better—"

"And then a nice quiet divorce in a few months? When all the heat's off?"

She looked at him, a long, slow gaze which curdled delicately toward sadness, and said, "Who's talking about divorce now? Who brought that one up just now?"

"Well, didn't you?"

"No. Do you want it? Is that what's on your mind now, Dick?"

"Yes," he said after a pause. "Yes, I think I want it. I think that that would be the best thing. Don't you?"

"Then we'll have to work it out for you if that's what you want."

"You didn't answer me! Do you want it or don't you?"

"Does it make any difference what I want at this stage of the game?"

"Yes, it makes a hell of a lot of difference!"

"You mean, you wouldn't go ahead with a divorce if I objected. That's just as magnanimous as all hell, isn't it?"

"I can't stand it," Martin said. "I can't stand this anymore. I deserve better than this." He had never said this before. In the context of the room it sounded definitive. "I just can't take it. Why should I?"

"Then we'll work out the thing any way you want it, Richard."

"How did this get started? All I did was mention Allen."

"I didn't want to talk about him. Is that all, Dick? I think that I'll take the car and drive off to see a movie or something. I don't feel like staying around here tonight. Maybe there's something good downtown."

"You don't have to run away."

"That's what I mean."

"I think Allen's crazy," he said. "I think the man is very sick. I can't get him out of my mind. I've been thinking about it all day and it's a terrible thing. That must be what's bothering me."

"I'm getting out of here now, Dick."

"Won't you talk to me? Won't you ever talk to me? Are you going to leave me alone here for a goddamned movie?"

"You don't understand," she said and she touched him once on the back of the neck and left him, leaving the door unlocked. He heard the car stumble from the driveway and then for a long time he sat alone in the apartment, looking at a bottle of scotch and thinking about Allen.

He almost thought of discussing the matter of Allen with someone else, someone of the medical staff, say, or at the higher echelon altogether. It would be interesting for him to bring up his point of view on the basis of his own experience (he would have a certain creditability about breakdowns) but on the other hand the thought of what could happen to him if he went up above with his suspicion that Allen was not competent was not pleasant. They could ask him some very tough questions about qualifications. So eventually he opened the bottle and began to work on it carefully, using the aftermath of the Allen drinks as the basis for putting it all together again and the scotch filled him with a slow, murky, passionless sense of release that began in his stomach and moved up to all the other levels of the body, leaving, as always, the groin intact. Nothing could touch the groin anymore. He wanted to see his wife but had passed out before she returned. It was surprising how he had never discovered until after the fact that all along he had the makings of a competent alcoholic.

Busby is the third man in the capsule. He will be the commander of the ship while the two others are on the Moon (which is putting a good face on the fact that he is the extraneous man in the expedition) and he will work the detonators for the seismic experiments planned on this voyage. It is, then, except for the business of the armaments, occupying Martin's old job, but he knows nothing of the man whatsoever. Busby's wife died in a peculiar way about a year ago and the man seems to be attached passionately to his daughter but these are not insights (merely data) and even with his newfound analytical sense he can do little with them. It is important to Martin, for some reason, that he try to clearly understand these men, that he get close to them in some psychological sense if no other and he thinks that after a fashion he may comprehend the other two ... but Busby is a mystery.

He hears vaguely that there was some talk of Busby dropping out of the project when his wife died, but this was quashed by the man's enormous rededication to the program; since then he has been one of the most absorbed and fanatical of all the astronauts and this more than anything else might account for his establishment in the control capsule during this voyage. They have had (even before Martin) some problems with the men in the control capsule; Martin was a really serious one, and this time they obviously want a man who will cause them as few difficulties as possible. Busby seems to be a proper choice since he will have somewhat less on his mind, possibly, than the other two. Martin would like to try knowing the man; he has had a couple of formal meetings with the three of them, of course, and Busby is the one he has tried to communicate with the most, but Busby, responding to everything stated with a dull, ponderous choice of words, a strange blankness of facial expression, seems to have very little to say and Martin can hardly force the issue.

It may only have to do with the missing wife. An astronaut without a wife is in a rather exposed position in this project and Busby, no less than would Martin in similar circumstances, has tried to depersonalize himself as much as possible. The daughter is a key, of course, but she is a routine, run of the mill type daughter, maybe a little slow for her age, no personality angle to her whatsoever until she came down with this broken leg and Martin can hardly look for insights there, broken legs hardly being psychological.

"I think that my job is really the most exciting and demanding of the three," Busby has said. "Just consider; I'll have the whole capsule to myself for forty-eight hours. All alone there; just imagine it, two days with the greatest view known to man" . . . but he has said all this with such absence of affect, such negative involvement that it is only possible to believe that on some profound internal level he feels very deeply. At least, Martin would like to think that he feels deeply; it would somehow be easier for him to bear this if he could, more or less, look *up* to the man who will do his job.

There is, as well, a new factor on this voyage. (Each voyage must add a little something new; Martin knows that this is called the Advancement of Science but in his post-flight thinking now wonders if it is only an illusion of progress granted to keep the appropriations advisers happy.) This ship is loaded with atomic devices which, on Busby's trigger, will lay down nuclear fire upon the Moon as the capsule breaks into orbit. The purpose of this is to induce earthquakes upon the Moon, planetary earthquakes of such violence that they may actually cause the satellite to shift somewhat from orbit and the degree to which the bombs alter the orbit will give the scientists great insights into the nature of apogee and trajectory and even the origin of Earth. (They will be able to measure all of these shocks through devices planted by Martin's crewmates, their last duty before a hasty exit.) It is understood that the explosives carried on board this ship will have more potential destructive power than any devices ever before tested and when he was once asked about them, Busby's solemnity broke for the only time and he said he guessed they did, that was why a cool hand was badly needed on their triggering devices.

"I wouldn't want to get excited and drop those babies at the wrong time," he said with a smile, "maybe get my heavenly bodies mixed up and drop them during the orbital escape here or maybe wait until we're back in the atmosphere. I guess that I won't carry along any government issue alcohol on *this* trip," and the comments provoked some laughter although Martin then had his single insight into Busby: he guessed that this was the kind of man who found cataclysm humorous, and this was as good an attitude as any because it meant that he had cultivated perspective somewhere along the line.

The business of his wife, it was understood, had settled him somewhat as death had a way of doing: the strange thing was that he and his wife had not gotten along very well and Martin has even heard rumors that Busby was one of the few adulterous astronauts in history . . . but after her death a good deal of shame had been mixed in with the loss and the man had firmed . . . up or down.

Martin supposes that he should get to know Busby; of all the men in the project, Busby may be the one to whom he has the most to say at this time, but it is just impossible. The men are deep into final training, have been since he came to his new job, and even if he were able to make connection, what could he tell Busby? No one could have told *him* anything; no one can yet and he supposes that the least that can be asked of any of them is that beyond the question of technical data they do no listening whatsoever. They have their own problems to work out; it will hardly do to make them emotional receptacles.

Martin has decided that when the trip is over, when the men are safely out of debriefing and press conferences and isolation and so on, when all of this has blown over and he can resign quietly, he will have a long talk with Busby and try to find out if the things that happened to him had tempted or afflicted the other man. Busby may have some interesting insights, even common experiences to share, and by that time Martin will feel free to speak. Now, however, there is nothing to do but stay organized and fulfill the requirements of his job and stay the hell out of any of the implications.

He sees Busby and himself at some time in the future. They are sitting somewhere, maybe a restaurant, drinking companionably. They are having martinis or perhaps screwdrivers and the glasses glisten in the sun which shines merrily through the windows overlooking their table. It is warm, dry, just a scent of summer in the air and they are pleasantly feeling the liquor although in no motor trouble whatsoever. Busby belches delicately, wipes a widower's hand across his mouth.

"Ah," he says, "ah, that was a rough son of a bitch, really a rough one."

"Then you had the same thing that I did," Martin will say. "You had troubles in orbit too. I wasn't alone. It was the condition."

"Of course," Busby will say. "Of course I did. Haven't we all? It's the nature of the game, the name of the orbit, the arc of the planet," and will give him a brother's look, a widower's tap, a small, stinging clasp in the warm restaurant and Martin will understand at last that there is no shame in it, no problem whatsoever, Busby his friend and brother has freed him forever and they will drape their arms around one another, put their faces together and begin to sing long, slow, whooping songs of space while outside the sun darkens in the afternoon and all the noises of the cafe are gentle, bright, tinkling as background to their ringing serenade. Busby his brother, his familiar, his extension, his idol, his ideal, the widower Busby releasing him at last.

Busby the adulterer.

Screw this, Martin says, lying stiff in his bed in the middle of the night, *screw it*, *screw it*, and finds that he is crying.

VIII

Get inside me, Richard Martin, she had moaned in the density of his car and he had floated over her, desperate, seeking the warm, red connection at the bottom of her but he had been blind, fumbling, frantic, and for an instant had thought that he could not find her, an intimation of shrinking and retreat coming over him, a terror that she would look down and see the secret of his doom but then, somehow, through all the chambers of clothing he had made it, wedged himself into her, and it had been all right, all right, everything fine.

Well, it had been workable anyway, that is: moving up and down like a clumsy marionette perched on her . . . and at the moment of discharge there had been a disconnection, a tearing free, and he thought that he could see everything, the totality of it hammered out against the rasp of his breath. It was near, sex brought it nearer than it had ever been before, sex with her anyway, it had never seemed so easy, if unreachable. Ah God, he had murmured and plunged into her although drained, God.

Good, good, she had come back at him and he had thought that he had pleased her . . . but much later it occurred to him that she might only have said *good* because she thought that he had said it and in any event it was over. He could not ask her; he would never know.

It had been a short courtship and he had fucked her only that one time before they were married; she was afraid of pregnancy, close quarters, involvement. What they had must be saved until they were married. She hated motels and was uncomfortable in cars. Cars made her feel like an extension of the machinery. All of this came out when he tried to fuck her for the second time two days after the first, and he accepted her objections. What else could he do? He wanted to see the answer again, hovering over her; if he had to get married to do it that was worthwhile. And anyway, she was compromising, she did go down for him instead, she was willing to go down for him or use her hands or any of that crap, just as long as they were definitely engaged and he didn't press the issue of fucking too hard. That there might be some other significance to her refusal to fuck had not hit him until many years later (in the capsule as a matter of fact) and by that time everything had gone out of the marriage as well so what the hell, why bother thinking about it? What was done was done.

It was a good philosophy and could carry you a long, long way, but since the Accident he had been doing more thinking, too much thinking, thinking above what he was really geared to handle and he found himself going back to a lot of things now that were finished. Not that it did him any good of course or harm for that matter either.

And not that he had wanted that badly at the time to change her mind. It was easier to blame the car, the motels, the pregnancy and the moral premise for what they were failing to do. You could skirt fear forever that way if you found enough things to blame. If you kept those objects in the mind at all times, you could even confuse them utterly with the central stuff and get mad at them and that could be a hell of an advantage.

IX

Busby, Davis and Allen have a final conference with the press before their debarkation on the morning hence. The conference is granted after all; it seems to have been kept indefinite only so that it would not be taken for granted. As a result, there is no television coverage and only a relatively small number of reporters are present for the conference.

As usual, they sit behind glass shielding. It has long since been pointed out that this provides no protection against contamination nor is contamination likely in such circumstances. Still, this provides a nice aseptic overlay to the situation and enables Davis, the sociologist, to make several wry remarks about the segregation factor, which always seems to take place in the presence of the unknown.

"It's a great opportunity," Davis is saying. "You see, what you've got in one of these flights, of course, is an archetypal stress situation with a good deal of social compression and it will be interesting to see how the patterns develop. Interacting with them all the time as a member of the situation, of course, so that there will be less distancing than usual. Having gone through this once before, I think that I'm in a good position to refine what I know to an even higher level."

"You mean," Allen says with an inquisitorial smile, turning slightly on his chair, "that I'm a pattern? And that Colonel Busby is a pattern and that you, the scientist among us, are both patterns as well? Just figments of sociology? That doesn't sound very promising to me, reducing people to charts. In fact, it sounds quite depressing. Of course, I've received customary warnings about sociologists and shouldn't take this seriously."

"No," Davis says quickly, before a question can come in; the press being none too eager anyway. "You've got it wrong. We aren't patterns, Commander. We *make* patterns; you always have configurations in human relationships totally apart from the personnel involved. I didn't mean in any way to imply that dehumanization exists. The human factor is paramount. That's why we have manned space flights in the first place, to get people out there."

"I know sociologists," Allen says, drumming his fingers on the table. "Yes indeed, I certainly do. I've heard a lot of reports about you people. You've got to be controlled."

"But you're not following, Commander," Davis says with a near-pedagogical air—as if he is trying to make some final, central point. "Really, try to understand me here. You've got to understand that we're getting right down to the basic behavioral situation, an archetype in fact: three men already well acquainted locked up in an enclosed, almost self-sufficient sub-society on a mission containing peril and doubt. Why, the religious overlay alone is fascinating! Trinity, you understand, and the similar archetypes. You can pull raw data out of this which could keep a foundation going for a hundred years."

"Do you consider this mission perilous, Colonel Davis?" someone asks from the rear. The men shift uneasily behind the gassline. Martin, in the front row, sees a slow cast of rage appear and then diminish in Allen's face.

He tries to make some kind of restraining gesture which Allen but none of the others will catch but finds himself instead clumsily waving his arm in such a way that the reporters near him in the row turn and look at him with some interest.

"Not perilous," Martin finds himself mumbling with a lunatic smile. "Not perilous at all. Certainly safe. Highly safe." The reporters shrug and make a few notes. They have never been terribly interested in him, which is all for the better.

"Well," Davis says carefully, "well, any voyage in which men and equipment are traveling a quarter of a million miles must be considered somewhat dangerous. Of course you've got a highly controlled situation here and the odds against disaster are enormous. Probably, statistically, going to the Moon is safer than driving my car to the grocery store. That isn't the question for a moment. But you must consider the question of archetypes."

"I don't understand from archetypes," the reporter says and there are giggles. "What's so archetypal about this?"

"I can't explain," Davis says. "I mean, there's some area of controversy here; if you find the view objectionable I'm not going to try to convert you. *Potentially*, there's a dangerous situation—*potentially* it's perilous—you've got to be dealing with a good amount of fear latent in any man who would undertake this mission. It's a question of how the fear is controlled. Maturity is sublimation in fact and so on. But now I seem to be going off at tangents which aren't particularly interesting and all of this is highly opinionated material anyway. Sociology is not yet an exact science; if we're lucky it may never be."

"I'm not afraid," Busby says, looking down at the table. "As long as we're on the issue of fear I want to make it quite clear that it doesn't figure whatsoever in my case."

"Colonel Davis, as a matter of fact, seems to be suggesting that *he* is afraid," Allen says. There is a pure, dead instant of silence; it hangs in the room and Allen catches it, acknowledges it, decides to ride over it in another way.

"Personally, I'm scared to death," he says and there is some laughter. "Of course they won't let me back down now. There's too much money invested to let a backup sneak in at this late date.

Now, if Colonel Davis and I had been discussing this three *weeks* ago there might have been some hope, but not now, unfortunately."

The reporters seem to find this humorous; there is more laughter although it is well contained. Martin slumps down, lets the laughter wash over him, wonders exactly what the hell Allen is up to. "If I had done it three weeks ago, they could have slotted Martin right into my spot and given *me* those press releases. But now it's just too late," Allen says and gives Martin a quick, piercing look which brings the two of them to attention in their seats.

Martin feels himself shaking with rage, a need to smash not far away from him, but then, as the Commander's glance turns distant and abstract, beginning to tumble into itself, Martin understands that Allen probably meant nothing whatsoever by the remark and that this man is functioning at another level entirely. The press materials clatter in his hand; he folds them and tries to slide them inconspicuously into a side pocket. One of the worst aspects of the job seems to be that documents are always being carried around, documents which are never used but for some reason must always be at hand. There is no telling when someone will want yet another press release or a list of the heroes of the project in the past. He wishes the conference were over; the room is becoming warm and there seems to be even more purposelessness to this conference than to his own, four months ago, when absolutely no one wanted to talk to the man who would remain in orbit.

"What will it feel like, Colonel Busby?" somebody asks perversely enough on the heels of this, "to be all alone in that capsule for two days while the others are on the Moon and all the attention will be focused on them? Do you have any plans to pass the time?"

This question has been asked at every conference since the pattern of Moon flights was set; even he had gotten this one perfunctorily and its recurrence means only that things are down again into a normal pattern, routine taunting that is, but Martin feels again a slow, perilous rage working through him; he would like to do something explosive to end the conference.

(His own response to the question had been that he was going to lay out a hell of a lot of solitaire. At some earlier point in the history of the project this might have been considered a fairly witty or at least disarming answer but ever since one of the men, a couple of years ago, had said that he planned to use the time to try and hustle all the ass that the agency smuggled into these flights, there had been no real topper. The monitors on the telecast—this had been at the continuing period of interest when the pre-flight conferences were still carried on the networks—had managed to catch the remark on the seven-second lag and knock it right out, but it had been recorded by some five hundred reporters, many of whom had laughed, and it had worked its way in inference into most of the unauthorized reports of the mission. The man, alas, had left months later under strained circumstances and was now doing private public relations work for a large male cosmetics firm but it had been a good try: there were very few in the project who had not been amused by it. Under other circumstances, a wonderful scatology and parochial wit might have come out of the progress of the project but it was set up all wrong for this kind of thing and the appropriations situation had not been good for so many years that the troubles looked permanent. A great loss to literature, of course.)

Busby, for some reason, seems to have taken the remark head-on and seems even a trifle disconcerted. "I don't think that's a fair question," he says. "The man in orbit is absolutely crucial. He may well be the most important of the three. In addition to having the responsibility for commanding the capsule, he must keep the support systems going, maintain the environment in the absence of the others, and remain at readiness for emergency maneuvers in case difficulties are encountered during exploration."

"Difficulties! Tell me, isn't all of that done by computer anyway?"

"There's a computer monitoring, certainly. But there is also an automatic override in case of potential loss to the integrity of the system. Which could happen at any time whatsoever."

"Has it ever happened?"

"Of course it's happened! It's happened too many times already."

"What I'm trying to say is during the Moon orbit has there ever been a breakdown in the support system?"

"So what!" Busby says loudly. "Read your informationals. It could happen at any time. Just because something hasn't yet happened doesn't mean it never will. This is serious business, quite serious. The Moon isn't a trip across town, you know, no matter what the Commander says. He's entitled to his view but I'm entitled to mine."

"Do you think that disaster lurks, Commander Allen?" the reporter says. "Or, as Colonel Busby puts it equally colorfully, do you think that this flight is indeed 'serious business'?" The reporter has a rather pleased expression but mixed with the pleasure is a hint of querulousness; if he has uncovered something it would not be the proper circumstance in which to emerge with something serious. These press conferences are not slanted toward that purpose, not at all.

"I've said no," Allen says stolidly. "I've said that the whole mission strikes me as rather routine. Let me try to make myself clear if I may. This is a research project, not a dangerous exploration, and I think that the more quickly we attempt to deglamorize this process and put it into perspective, the more long-range value we are going to have. It's time that everyone grew up: the project, the reporters, the public. We can no longer, obviously, entice people into listening to us because of the possibility of danger. We have to make it on accomplishment, on worth, on the meaning we can bring into their lives."

"I see," the reporter says. "Would that be a disagreement?"

"What?"

"I said, there seems to be a disagreement between you and Colonel Davis on this issue. You seem to have rather opposed views of the mission: its purposes and its outcome."

"I don't follow you," Allen says rather quizzically, his fine, high forehead seeming to come to a faint sheen. "I just don't see what you're driving at right this minute, young man. I really don't."

"Well, different outlooks," the reporter says hesitantly. "A different point of view. I didn't mean anything by it. It isn't very important, I'm sure that it's of no importance at all."

Martin feels that at this point he should stand and say something. He definitely has something to say and it is his right to intervene. He has, after all, been the matchmaker, so to speak. He has introduced the three men to the press; it will be he who will terminate the conference at a time he takes to be propitious. They have been talking for only twenty minutes but the time could be propitious right now. Then again, maybe it is not. He does not want to give the press the impression that the three men are being held back or protected in any way. On the other hand, there is a nastiness of temper to this particular conference which he has not noted in any previously.

Delicate, delicate considerations! And he has no equipment. His own perspective may have been altered by what has happened to him; his judgment might even be faulty. Then too, if the decision as to when to terminate the conference had any real significance, it probably would not have been given to him in the first place.

He is thinking all of these things over, without particular cogency, and is almost on the point of standing anyway when Davis says, "You're bound to have differences of opinion in any situation set up like this. Why worry about any of it? I'm sure that the three of us have bought the same objectives."

"What's your position on the danger of the flight? Do you think that there's any risk-factor in the equation now?"

Davis shakes his head and says, "I'm a sociologist. That's my division; I can't comment on the hard sciences. It's the hard sciences which must control the safety of a mission. I'm sure that there's very little risk though or I wouldn't be along. Sociologists are not exactly in the front lines, you know."

There is more laughter and Martin decides suddenly that he has had enough of the press conference. He will exercise his power and call it off. He is tired of the press, tired of comments, tired of a certain edge of terror which he suspects lies under all of the questions but which the press, no less than the astronauts, seems interested only in titillating without exploration. He has had quite enough of the press in any case; it is impossible, even after having dealt with them for weeks, to manage any sense of individuation. They all posture the same way, talk the same bullshit questions, address everything with the same sullen hostility. Whatever they are after can have nothing to do with any reality which he has been conditioned by terror to understand.

Martin stands ponderously and picks up the remote amplifier which has been lying next to his chair. "Thank you all very much," he says. "The conference is now over."

"Now let's just wait a second," a reporter says quickly. The reporter, as a matter of fact, seems to be the same one who was asking questions of the men about danger and who yesterday was pressing Martin; Perkins his name is and Martin realizes that he is afraid of him. This is the only individuated reporter and that is not exactly their role. "What are you cutting us off for? There are some additional questions which I'm sure we all want to ask."

"As you were advised at the beginning, this conference cannot take precedence. Scheduling is tyrannical, gentlemen; we must defer to it. The crew must now return to its quarters to face more training tomorrow; final preparations are well in process—"

"I don't buy that," the reporter named Perkins says. "I don't buy it because every time we edge into something interesting with anyone here we get cut off."

"No you don't."

"Yes we do! Now this has been going on for a long, long time, this nonsensical manipulation, but I don't see any reason why we have to cater to you anymore. We're doing *you* people a favor by being here. No one's interested in this stuff anymore, can't you get that through your heads? It's dead meat! If it wasn't kept alive somehow—"

Two old guards come to flank the reporter, look him over quizzically. Standing by the door with unlit pipes they had looked curiously effective, but in action they do not sustain that impression. In fact, they seem confused as they look up at him with bulbous old eyes full of complaint.

"Look here," Martin says gently enough. "This is not fair. No one is covering up at all. You're just trying to twist things around to suit a certain interpretation and I don't know what you're after."

"I don't work for the *standard* press," Perkins says harshly. "I work for a magazine with a circulation of three hundred thousand subscribers. Subscribers *only*—we don't put up with the newsstand garbage that permits only lies to be told. These people, our subscribers, want answers. That's why they buy us, that's why they resubscribe, that's why they retain loyalty to us, because we give them answers. Now if we're not prepared to get at the truth here—"

"What answers do you want?" Allen says quizzically, rubbing his palms against one another and looking side-wise at Davis with a tiny smile. "I don't understand you, sir. What haven't we provided that you seem to be missing?"

"I'm missing the whole damned picture," the reporter says as the guards straggle back toward the wall, holding their pipes like guns. Maybe they think the pipes *are* guns. "Now you people are singing a lot of folk songs but the essential story is missing here. That goddamned ship is going up with enough nuclear armaments to destroy a bloody continent. You're putting enough fissionables in this thing, maybe, to blow up a *planet* and yet no one has yet asked what kind of controls are being inserted on this ship. What happens if you get socked by something in space and the ship blows up, huh? And all this happens within the Earth's orbit. What if one of you guys goes crazy and decides to take over the world? What if the *agency* goes crazy and decides that they can use the three of you up there to blackmail for more goods? What I want to know is who's on the trigger? What's the point? Who's running this show? And what do you want to bomb the Moon for? Hasn't it got enough problems? I thought it was an inert body."

The questions do not provoke a cataclysm. To the contrary, there are only scattered mumbles through the room; Perkins is screwing up the chance of an early exit. Looking to his right and left, Perkins seems to grasp this and laughs, not entirely pleasantly. "I see," he says. "I see what kind of system you cats have."

Allen leans forward quickly and says, "I don't quite know what answers you want. You're obviously out just to create a certain rampaging mood of fantasy."

"Rampaging mood of fantasy," Perkins says. "I like that. That's a good one. That's what you can call your whole program."

"Let me finish. Or do you want to take over here? We're taking some fissionables on board, that is correct. No secret was ever made of that. How could you know if the agency didn't tell you?"

"You can't conceal the truth."

"Nonsense, son. Anything could be concealed. There are certain seismic experiments planned which will be conducted by laying down nuclear fire upon the Moon when we exit. The seismic stresses caused by the detonations will be measured and will lead to a heightened understanding of the Moon and, hopefully, of the Earth. That is the reason, the only reason for these fissionables on board."

"So what if there's a malfunction? What if there are problems on lift-off or in space and that stuff gets hot? It would be attracted to the largest body near it, now wouldn't it? I want to know what kind of controls you have—"

"You don't understand science," Allen says gently. "People who don't understand science tend to hate it and they can always get an audience composed of fear. No, Colonel, let me handle this," Allen says, noting that Martin has put the loudspeaker near his mouth. "Let me talk. I can handle this perfectly."

"Go on," Perkins says, "go on, call off the press conference. That's the point, isn't it?"

"No," Allen says. "Look." He pauses, shakes his head, seems to think a minute and then draws himself together. "You people—I mean the kind of people who you say are your subscribers and followers—have misunderstood this project from the first and you look at it with unrelieved hostility. You're interested in dealing with it only in terms of exploitation, negative publicity so to speak, and that is as close as you want to get to understanding."

"Pompous," the reporter says. "Pompous."

"Let me finish, son. There's something basic here. Now, you're entitled to your point of view, of course. No one is censoring your publication and you are free to think and write as you please. But you won't do any thinking."

"*You* won't think," Perkins says. "No one in this project in ten years has given an instant's thought as to what is really going on here."

"I disagree. There has been a lot of thought. Now, if you had done any investigation at all, minimum reporting to the extent that you had read the press releases which I'm sure Colonel Martin has given you—"

"Lies! It's all a pack of crap! Nicely packaged, colorful crap out of the taxpayer's money!"

"—You would have seen that the radioactives are in a state of total inactivity until they are actually fired, and that the atomic piles are set up in such a fashion that they could only be triggered by an intricate series of actions which are totally within the control of the operator. And unless this whole complicated action-cycle is completed, the fissionables will remain harmlessly in their shells, in an inert state, and will be utterly harmless."

"All of you talk the same."

"Only to an outsider, son."

"It all sounds very neat. It sounds very neat and explicit, but how do *we* know what your agency really has in mind? Maybe you're going to go up into an Earth-orbit and blackmail. That's what I think! We know you're in trouble; you can't put it over on us anymore! We know that the whole bubble burst."

Busby stands, palms flat to the table, leaning slightly, swaying, and says, "I'm the one who's operating those armaments, you son of a bitch."

"I know that."

"You know that? You say one more word about me or this agency or my integrity and I'll break your neck. I've had all of this that I'm going to listen to, ever. The hell with it."

Davis makes a restraining gesture, whispers something to Busby, but the man does not seem to hear. "No, no," he says, "there's no reason to take this. We don't have to put up with it, not anymore, and bastards like this aren't going to bait me. Now you get the hell out of this room before I decontaminate myself and kill the whole trip by going over to your chair and laying you out cold."

"All right," Martin says through the amplifier. "All right now, that's all, this press conference is over, no more questions." He turns the volume to full hype, repeats *No more questions!* and the reporters, looking blankly at one another, murmur and move slowly toward the rear of the room.

Perkins is surrounded by a few others who do not look cordial but then Perkins does not look cordial himself; he is staring at Busby, his mouth drawn into a hard line, a peculiar malevolence darting from the tiny eyes and Martin, already feeling detached from the situation, feels fright.

It is not a fear which has anything to do with Perkins; Perkins is out of it utterly. No, the fear comes from a different direction. Martin finds that he is grasping the loudspeaker in a hand become white with trembling; he finds that his breath is uneven. The amplifier feels oppressive and he hurls it from him, turning to watch the three men as they stand to leave. The amplifier, still at full, hits the floor with a terrifying smash and they leap.

"Wait!" he cries, and they turn, two of them anyway . . . the third, Busby, seems to be in some highly abstracted state, picking at the edges of strands of hair, running his other hand down creases in his pants, and Martin feels the slow foolishness coming over him. He wants to talk to them somehow, make a point clear, but he does not know what he wants to say and then too there is no way that he can join them; they are to be segregated from the possibility of infection.

"Forget it," he says, moving a wrist awkwardly, "forget it, it's nothing," and the three file out, leaving the bright haze of the isolation chamber winking in its emptiness. Like a capsule, eviscerated. He wanted to talk to them, he had something to say, but they are already gone and under the rules he cannot touch them until weeks after they return.

They are out of reach and then—

he feels the curse, the contaminants on his palms, the bright web of infection he carries like an insect, slashes of infection moving like insects through him and he feels a stab of illness, some central apprehension of his own terrible weakness which causes him to double over and retch but only very quietly and then into the palm of his hand, there being no reason whatsoever to claim the attention of the press which also knows of his stain, the isolation-producing stain, all of them know—

It's space-sickness, he would tell them if anyone noticed what was happening, just a little bit of the old spaceman's burden, carried back from the Moon. We old space-loggers, we learn to put up with a little bit of taint. It's the price of the stars, isn't it?

X

The compulsion had come on him gradually. In the earliest stages of the flight it had been little more than a whimsy: WHAT WOULD THEY SAY IF—; later on, it had been an earnest questioning: NOW WHAT WOULD THEY DO TO ME IF—; and then, finally, in the last stages it had been—

—unbearable; the men down on the Moon; he on the other side and out of contact and the button with the retrofire had glinted at him in the darkness of the capsule whispering its message in a small but manic voice.

COME ON, the button said, WHAT THE HELL, MUST DO IT, TAKE A CHANCE. THEY'LL CALL IT TECHNICAL MALFUNCTION ANYWAY AND YOU'LL BE CALLED TWICE A HERO FOR MANAGING TO ESCAPE WITH YOUR LIFE. DO IT, COME ON, NOTHING TO LOSE.

"Be reasonable," he said to the button (in the early stages he was still trying to be reasonable; even to the very end he was still doing his best to act like a logical man), "that wouldn't work at all; don't you understand that the damned thing is linked up to the computers, and they'd know right away what I had done? They'd arrest me the minute I landed and I would be the greatest criminal in history, greater even than the barbarians because look at the distance I had gone to murder." He had twisted and clasped his fingers, holding them in his lap, sometimes *sitting* on them; anything to keep his hands away from the button—

—which knew everything about him, knew him right down to the core; COME ON, it said to him, SO WHAT THE HELL IF THEY DID KNOW WHAT YOU'D DONE, SO THEY FIND OUT, SO WHAT? THEY CAN'T DO A THING TO YOU, NOT A SINGLE THING BECAUSE THEN THE WHOLE STORY WOULD COME OUT AND THEY'D PROBABLY KILL THE APPROPRIATIONS OR SOMETHING AND THEY CAN'T KILL YOU BECAUSE THAT WOULD LOOK TOO SUSPICIOUS SO THEY'LL JUST PENSION YOU OFF TO SOME EASY JOB SOMEWHERE AND KEEP YOU CLOSE UNDER WRAPS. YOU WOULDN'T SUFFER HARDLY AT ALL. ANYWAY, FORGET THOSE TWO BASTARDS. THE HELL WITH THEM. WHAT DO THEY MEAN TO YOU? THEY GO OFF PLAYING ON THE MOON AND LEAVE YOU UP HERE IN THE CAPSULE ALL ALONE. THEY GET ALL THE COVERAGE WHILE YOU HAVE TO SIT LIKE A LUMP IN THIS LOUSY CAPSULE AND WAIT FOR THEM TO COME BACK. WHAT THE HELL DO THEY MATTER? THEY DON'T CARE IF YOU LIVE OR DIE JUST AS LONG, JUST AS LONG AS THE CAPSULE STAYS ALOFT. LISTEN, THEY DESERVE IT. YOU KNOW THEY DESERVE IT. COME ON, the button said, and seemed to palpitate slowly before him. COME ON, WHAT THE FUCK. YOU ONLY LIVE ONCE. GIVE US A LITTLE PUSH AND SHOW THEM THAT THEY CAN'T TREAT YOU LIKE DIRT.

The stinking button, but it knew everything, knew just how to get to him: LISTEN, YOU'VE BEEN TRAINED ALL YOUR LIFE TO DO SOMETHING LIKE THIS. THIS IS WHAT IT WAS ALL FOR.

"No," he said, "no!" But that had been in the early part of the orbit; he had gone back into darkside three more times and each time the button was a little more insistent, a little more persuasive, and by the middle of the fourth he did not understand anymore why he should not go ahead and do what it asked. After all, it was so reasonable, it was a *reasonable* button, that was the hell of it; it was only asking him to do something that he had wanted to do for a long time himself and if the button—

—cared to make the case then so much the better, it took some of the responsibility away from him. Hell, it was hardly his fault at all when you looked at it that way; they had no business putting him in orbit with such a seductive—

—button! if they wanted him to perform reasonably. Swinging in and out of darkness four times: on the light side exchanging communications with the base (everything in shape here), banter with the men (they were scrambling like rabbits over the surface of the Moon, they had found something that looked like diamonds; one of them had left his wife's jewelry in a crater to give her a little bit of eternity; one of them reminded the other of a clumsy diver about to one-and-a-half), instructions with control; the essence of reason, competence in the capsule (everything in shape here) and then, oh God (everything in shape here, no problems looking back toward the dark shift, waiting for some company), back to darkside where the button emerged from its shroud and began to talk—

—to him again. COME ON, the button said, THEY'RE ALL SET UP FOR IT NOW. SEE HOW LITTLE THEY CARE FOR YOU? SEE THE CONTEMPT THEY HAVE? THEY JUST TAKE YOU FOR GRANTED. THEY TAKE FOR GRANTED THAT YOU'LL PUT UP WITH THIS FUCKING SHIT. WELL, YOU DON'T HAVE TO DO IT ANYMORE. GIVE US A LITTLE JAB AND LETS HAVE SOME RETROFIRE.

"Oh God, you son of a bitch," he said on the third orbit when they were really deep into it and he was no longer capable of fighting off the suggestions, "you can't take retrofire from darkside, we'll fly right into the—

—sun." YOU STUPID BASTARD, the button had said but with a caress to its voice. They had adopted the relationship, already, of old, twisted lovers. YOU DON'T HAVE TO WORRY ABOUT THAT AT ALL, YOU OLD THIEF, YOU JUST WAIT UNTIL YOU GET INTO THE NEAR CYCLE AND THEN YOU MAKE A NICE LEVEL FIRE. WHY DON'T YOU USE A LITTLE CIRCUMSPECTION? YOU WERE TRAINED TO THINK THESE THINGS OUT ON YOUR OWN. WHY DO I HAVE TO TELL YOU EVERYTHING? I CAN'T BE HERE FOREVER, YOU KNOW. I HAVE SOME RESPONSIBILI- TIES OF MY OWN. THERE ARE A WHOLE LOT OF OTHER THINGS I HAVE TO DO BESIDES SPEND MY TIME JAB- BERING WITH YOU SO MAKE SOME CALCULATIONS AND SHOW SOME COMMON SENSE.

"But you don't understand," he pointed out, "it's all com- puter calculated, the perigee, when I have to hit it to make the proper entry. The only thing that's voluntary is the pushing; if I miss we're really in the soup, because it's all controlled."

SHOW THEM, the button had said, unpersuaded, in its merry, determined voice, SHOW THEM THAT YOU ARE A MAN AND NOT A ROBOT. SHOW THEM THAT THEY CAN'T PUSH A MAN LIKE YOU AROUND WITH THEIR GODDAMNED SILLY ORDERS AND ARROGANCE BUT THAT YOU'VE GOT A MIND OF YOUR OWN AND YOU CANNOT BE TRIFLED WITH. JUST TAKE OFF, MAKE THE PRETTY FIRE. THEY'LL TALK YOU DOWN SOMEHOW: THEY DON'T WANT TO LOSE THE GODDAMNED SHIP. THEY'LL SCRAMBLE FOR WHATEVER THEY CAN GET.

By the time he had finished the fourth revolution he knew that he could not hold out much longer. Now they were in brightside again, two short hours of it and then clamber back to the dark and he knew that the next time around he would prob- ably do it. He wanted to do it. He could not resist the button any longer. On that revolution he leaned against the bulkhead with his full weight, trying to pin his hands, his—

—*hands*, so that he could not reach to grasp, but his hands, his goddamned hands kept scurrying below his beltline, making frantic, independent gestures, the way that in different circumstances twenty-five years ago they would try to tell him to masturbate. Oh, how he had loved to masturbate! Well that had been a long time ago, no need to look back on it, with the BUTTON glinting before him, his lips becoming wet, his forehead distending and bulging like a prick. His body felt like a prick, tumescent toward some dreadful conclusion. Beneath—

—him the men caroled for the season, laid down marks for future crews, wished him well in jest and song and spirit and harmony and he wanted to kill them but they were too far for such immediacies, that would have taken too long. There was something much closer at hand, it was the BUT, it could do much BUTTO, could much better BUTTON do to them. His fingers trembled, he could feel them reaching toward the B the BUTTO the damned BUTTON, his body, tumescent, seeming to enlarge mercilessly, massively, fill every crevice of the ship so that he could not move. DO IT said the BUTTON and as the men began to sing a duet something cracked through, some understanding of what was happening—

—dancing on the Moon
In this night of June—

—not that understanding had anything to do with it and he screamed through thin layers of wall, two hundred and forty-three thousand miles down the tube. "Oh God!" he shrieked, "oh God help me, please help me now!" and bent over—

GOD HELPS THOSE WHO HELP THEMSELVES, said the BUTTON. NOTHING VENTURED NOTHING GAINED.

—from the waist, putting his hands between his legs and clasping his thighs like a BUTTO like a lover. BUTTON. "No, no, I don't want to do it!" he cried and hung there, waiting for the words that BUTTO would save him, knowing that even if they came BUTTON and if he were saved it would be too late. It had nothing to do with what was going on here today. It went much further back, further back, further in to—

YOU SILLY SON OF A BITCH, said the BUTTON petulantly but with massive conviction, YOU SILLY SON OF A BITCH YOU'RE GOING TO SCREW UP THIS WHOLE BEAUTIFUL THING BETWEEN US IF YOU DON'T WATCH YOURSELF YOU'D BETTER SHOW SOME CONTROL, said the—

—BUTTTO—

—BUTTON—

XI

In bed, that night, he tries once again to make love to his wife.

He is determined that this time he will take her. The connection will come face-to-face, lip-to-lip, and he will not stop until he has drawn from her a yielding cry. Again, like dough, she comes against him at this touch, molds herself heavily to him and opens herself silently. This seems to be a continuation of the terms of the Agreement which has been worked out since his return from the hospital: he will take, she will submit, there will be no dialogue, she will remain underneath him until he is finished. She will depart. It is a satisfactory agreement, at least in terms of his being drained out, and probably fairer than he could ask in terms of the way that she must really feel but he will have none of this anymore. He knows that he must force her to connect; it is something which he can hold against her later.

"No," he says, then, with a fingertip she urges him inside, "no, no, not so soon," and begins to work on her instead in the old way. He prowls the surfaces of her body with lips and tongue, his hands dropping to brush her now and then, establish positioning, force conditions upon her body. She pushes against him, resists, then collapses into an acceptance more deadly than struggle and moving lower upon her he feels that he has broken through to something within her but as he turns to look at her he finds her eyes wide and pitiless, unyielding, years in those eyes, her nostrils flaring slightly with the effort of controlled exhale.

"Are you finished?" she says. "Is that it and are you quite finished now?"

"Cunt," he says, "bitch," and bites her on the stomach. She recedes beneath him, all flesh and moisture, a small cry pinging the night.

"Are you finished now?" she says again when he looks at her and he feels a killing rage, an urge to buck and strike against her, damage her irreparably, make her pay too . . . but that, as he has been faithfully promised by the competent medical staff, that too passes and he confronts her, eye to eye in the heavy night, stumbles over her, oozes rage from his mind and tries to force from her by exertion what he could not by cunning, moving in and out of the slick damned walls (surely, if she were feeling nothing, she could not be so damp; surely he must believe that on some level he is getting past her), grinding himself into jellylike damp and then arching past desire into a cold determination to make her come but looking down at her again—

—seeing her inert on the pillow, head tossed to one side, her eyes open and pitiless toward the wall he feels helplessness, pointlessness behind the necessity and as he hovers so he shrinks, his prick retarding in tempo to his strokes until he is tottering upon insufficiency, ground to dust underneath him. He crawls out of her falling heavily to one side, his hands picking the sheet, cursing. She says nothing. Her breathing becomes regular. He has demolished himself and she is asleep beside him.

"Why?" he says, meaning to say more, but the question is enough. "Why?"

"It had to be, that's why," she says, her voice already blurred. "Don't make me get up. You made it that way. It's all your fault, the whole thing. I want to sleep."

"No it isn't. I didn't do it."

"Yes you did."

"I didn't. It was beyond me."

"No it wasn't. Everything was you. I want to sleep, Richard. It's very late, terribly late, I'm exhausted."

"I wanted you."

"So?"

"I said, I wanted you."

"You had me, didn't you?"

"I didn't have you. I didn't have any part of you. Can't you feel?"

"Only when I want to."

"You did everything."

"It was all your own fault. You can't blame me for a single thing anymore. What you wanted, you got. I'm not to blame for anything."

"You really don't care anymore, do you?" he says. "It just isn't there."

"You're wrong," she says. Her voice is soft, arching toward sleep murmur, she is getting away from him after all. "You're all wrong, you still think in terms of thingness. There is no thingness, only feeling. Dick, you must let me sleep; I need sleep. No more, please."

"I don't understand," he says. "I don't understand a single thing that has happened to me, not ever. None of it makes any sense."

"Then you'll have to work it all out for yourself. I can't work for you anymore. If you want me you can try again but short of that, leave me alone. I don't want to talk. I cannot talk anymore."

"Don't," he says, "don't," and moves on top of her again; this time he closes his eyes and thinks only of necessity: the necessity to finish. He must make come out of himself, spoon himself into her and then he will sleep, will find some peace. Thinking: he thinks of valves, locks, pressure gaps, slow pressures and changes in space and his tool, distended at last to enormous size, lodges into her like an excess growth. He pumps, grinds, wishes and—

—spits into her. He retracts. It is all quite separated from him. It is as if he has pulled a piece of machinery into place to perform a function and then, upon discharge, pushed it away. He is anesthetized, finished at last.

He can tell that he has come only from the damp in which his pubis now moves as he lurches toward a more comfortable position.

It has been this way since the Accident and if he could cry he supposes that he would do so, but crying seems purposeless. What does it have to do with anything? His wife asks him if everything is all right now and he says yes, composes himself for sleep. They might as well have never spoken. The sound of her breath curls over him as he circles into his own space and at the center of this sleep toward which he is spiraling is an understanding.

The understanding hits him like an uncoiled spring. It bounces all the way back from somnolence and tosses him into an uneasy wakefulness during which he finds himself clutching the covers, shaking.

He wonders if it has been the same way for her as well.

Has it been this way for her always? From the first time when she asked him to get in quickly, hoping, then, only to discover anesthesia again? Long, long before the Accident did she learn to live with her own disaster and that there was nothing below? And has the Accident which has done this now to him as well brought them closer together and in this closeness, this mutuality of understanding, made their lives unbearable . . . because all differences denied they are now pinned together in this emptiness forever? Is that *it*?

Oh boy.

Too much for Richard Martin. He is of simpler stock; he cannot understand psychology let alone enact it. He wanted to go to the Moon; that was his speed. The other stuff was too complicated.

Forget it. It all would have worked out the same, anyway. Think of *doppelgängers*, think of thieves in the night.

All the terrors seem to happen near sleep. The days are largely a winding in and out of this condition of semi-consciousness. But he really cannot take this anymore. He must sleep now. Tomorrow is the day of the launch. He will stand with the press while the ship staggers into space on a hundred screens lined through the briefing room. And then he must be on hand to advise the press through the period of the telecasts. The landing.

The exploration. The return to the capsule. The relaunch. The laying—

—down of nuclear fire. The re-entry. And the recovery. The litany is already ingrained, except for the nuclear fire, of course; a long time ago there might have been another way of looking at the problem of making the Moon but it is not circumscribed by schedule. It was all worked out long before they came and is unalterable. He is a responsible man; he will stay within the format at all times.

A responsible man. A responsible job. And when it is over, they will allow him to quit, unremarkably. That at least is to hope for.

Richard Martin, the astronaut who could not quite make it in orbit (but he tried, boys and girls, oh how he tried; even at the end he was still trying to do his job, screaming on the sea), slams his fist into the pillow, lets all the lines of his face collapse, and sinks then into an intermittent doze, his hands nevertheless clasped as if for prayer or mercy.

XII

He dreams the ship explodes during launch and the men fall out of it intact, beating at the air like swimmers, crying for recovery as they fall toward the Earth. "Save me!" cries Allen, "Save me!" cries Davis, "Me too!" says Busby but no provisions have been made for rescue and they fall to the pad, flatly, breaking their bones but not their flesh and then dissolve against the residue of the fire. The ship implodes above and settles back to Earth in the form of flowers. The flowers sift like birds and cover the inert forms of Allen, Busby and Davis. In the middle of all of this, the astronaut is standing, facing the press, trying to explain the true significance of this event. He forgets this dream.

XIII

He stays with the press during the launch and receives a word that the Director wants to see him. It has been a routine launch; some small leakage of gas retarded countdown for a hold at the tenth minute, but the leakage turned out to be from instrument breakdown and not in fact. (The instruments control the reference of the flight, though; there is simply no trifling with anything they have to say. If they call for jettison, one of the crew might have to go.) Busby, cramped in the pads and the uneasiest of the three, made some joke about the gas being a byproduct, maybe, of an excess of conversation, but there was no laughter, only a grunt from Allen who then said that despite this sound, everything remained in order. Davis began to hum the music of an obscene song which Martin knew but he did not look at the reporters nor they at him; all of them were fixated on the screens: screens throughout the room, screens to the side and above them, screens so that there was no possibility that they would miss any of the launch. The multiple screens had come in at the launch-before-last as a concession to the reporters who were afraid to go to the launch site.

At the seventh second the ship took power, at the third down it began to strain and at the first it became airborne. Martin, watching the screens closely, his first launch since the Accident, had a sudden image of implosion (having forgotten his dream), the ship gathering in upon itself in space and hardening to a series of small fragments gathering toward the Earth. He thought of the men lapsed into unconsciousness by the g-pressure and wondered why the blackout-on-launch was the one bit of information never offered the press. (Did they think that men could stand seven-gravity pressure without passing out? Did they think that you could come back to consciousness in a nausea which all the depressions could not eliminate? Did they think that any amount of training could ever cancel that out? Did they think that there were machines inside that capsule, just machines?) He brought his arms instinctively across his chest in the gesture of submission trained as the position for the launch, then, when the transmission began again, the ship out of the atmosphere and the men making jokes about the direction of their flight (going downrange toward the continental divide, Busby said), he felt himself lapse out of this suspension of catalepsy, shook his head, gathered his papers, looked around the room to see if anyone had observed his reaction and then left hurriedly by an inconspicuous exit.

The Director has advised him to report and since this will be his first encounter with the man since joining the project, Martin feels that it will probably be a good idea to be prompt. Then too, at that first encounter he had been one of twenty men, the latest group being taken in at the quarterly muster, and there was a certain intimacy lacking . . . which, in the case of dealing with the Director as he has come to understand him, was probably all for the best.

Martin passes through various levels of the center, moving through checkpoints and barriers, over a piece of ground, down a level, up a level, through a gate, finding no interference until he comes to the reception room of the Director himself. Outside there, for the first time, his credentials are checked by a guard with an empty face and enormous eyes who looks at him with loathing. "Martin, huh?" he says after looking through the various cards twice. "Is that your name?"

"It says so."

"Well, I'm still asking. I don't know anything," the guard says. "I just came in here last week; I don't know about nothing and it better stay that way."

"All right."

"I think I remember you, though. You used to be one of the astronauts, didn't you? The name sounds a little familiar."

"I was on the last mission."

"How could you be on the mission and standing here? That doesn't make sense."

"The mission before this. The last launch. Not this one."

"Oh," the guard says. "That's interesting. I don't really follow these things, you understand. I got no real interest."

He admits Martin to an enormous reception room behind whose desk sits a lieutenant in dress blues. The lieutenant looks at Martin with some interest and says, "Are you him?"

"Am I who?"

"Are you Richard Martin?"

"Yes," he says. "I was told that the Director wanted to see me."

"Then you're Richard Martin."

"I said that. I'm reporting for an appointment with the Director."

"That's interesting," the lieutenant says. He takes the phone up and talks quietly for a minute, then replaces it and says, "I guess you do have an interview. He's busy right now, though; you'll have to wait. It might be a long time."

"I don't know if I should wait too long. Maybe I should try another time; the press is around still and—"

"I wouldn't worry about that, Mr. Martin," the lieutenant says. "I have a feeling that the press can spare you. Stop taking yourself so seriously; cultivate a little perspective."

He picks up the phone again and begins to speak intensely to someone; perhaps he is continuing a conversation which Martin's entrance has interrupted and then again there may be something in the very technology of the system which Martin has missed. Maybe the lieutenant is wired into the ship and is calling instructions for the second-stage lift-off. He can only sit there, in the bare office on a straight-backed chair and while three men are hurled to the Moon, put up with whatever the Director has in mind for him.

It is strange to understand that this launch appears to have had no effect upon the lieutenant, no effect, for that matter, on any of the aspects of the project he has passed through on his way here. For all the difference that this launch has made, it might as well have been conducted routinely underground and broadcast as simulation. Of course, Martin understands that this is not like the old days, that the project has become irretrievably vast, that things are not quite as they once might have been . . . and that well over ninety percent of the employees or officials of the project have absolutely nothing to do with the progress of any given launch. They have their *own* cycles. Nevertheless, it is a disconcerting business to observe: during his own flight he had sustained the (at first pleasant) sensation that not only the world but the entire campus of the project was observing him closely, was organizing all routine around the observation. Maybe he would have been better off if he had understood from the beginning that no one cared; that for all the effect which the launch is having in these offices, they might as well have been engaged in some obscure driving test in another part of the country or the project in another branch of research altogether.

"Peculiar," Martin says and then is embarrassed to find that he has said this aloud. Things like this have been happening to him recently although only on occasion. The lieutenant looks at him quizzically. "Well, isn't it strange?" he says rather belligerently and finds that he is repressing a giggle. "All of it, very much so."

"What's that?" the lieutenant says without interest and takes another piece of paper from the side of his desk, examines it. "I don't really know what you're talking about."

"Well, there's just been a lift-off, but life yet goes on," Martin says. His voice fades into a mumble, he feels the smile becoming tense on his face. It does not seem that he has been making himself entirely clear.

"Why shouldn't it?" the lieutenant says. "Is there anything wrong with that procedure? Do you find it objectionable?"

"That's not what I meant. I was just a bit surprised that on the very day of the launch—"

"You misunderstand," the lieutenant says. "I'm completely administrative. I have nothing whatsoever to do with that other business and I don't even want to hear about it."

"All right."

"Is it necessary for you to talk?"

"What's that?"

"Because I'm pretty busy and I'd just as soon not be distracted. You may have to sit in this room for a while but that doesn't give you license to talk to me. I'd rather have an office of my own but not a chance."

"That's all right," Martin says, shifting a bit. "I didn't mean to disturb you."

"You people never mean, you just act," the lieutenant says. "Of course, that's all part of the problem, you know."

Then, for some time, nothing whatsoever happens. Martin leans back on the chair, willing himself into suspension. The lieutenant continues to look at forms and make occasional marks on them. Through the semi-soundproofing of the doors he thinks he can hear a clattering in the halls. On the other hand, he has no idea of what could be moving out there. The project has always been full of strange noises: unexpected explosions in the night would, in the early years, tumble him from bed gasping. There are rumors of huge nuclear reactors underneath the ground conducting detonation-tests and filling their bones with radiation but nuclear reactors or not, the project is full of the inexplicable.

After a good long time—fifteen minutes may have passed, maybe thirty—the intercom flashes on the lieutenant's desk. "You can go in now," he says. "Right through that door behind me. You don't need any escort now, do you?"

"I don't think so."

"Because sometimes you people have to be led by the hand. You'd be surprised how many don't quite know the way from here to there. Then too, I always retain the hope that we'll come up with a self-sufficient one sooner or later."

"Well, here he is," Martin says, moving past the lieutenant to the door. "The search is over." An idle urge to strike him comes almost absently. He would like to smash this lieutenant . . . but how can there be any profit in that? Besides, the lieutenant, seen from this closer perspective as he passes him, appears to be quite young: twenty-three or twenty-four at the most, and at the center of his soft, bright eyes is a light which might be deduced as panic or the sheerest madness. Martin realizes that the lieutenant may well be in the grip of forces at least as complex as those which seize him and the rage seems to drain away. "I can find my way around here pretty well," he points out. "You'd be surprised what kind of a sense of direction living in a capsule gives you. You can't get confused or you'll wind up on the wrong planet."

"Hah!" the lieutenant says. "I wouldn't talk about confusion, Martin, if I were you. I really wouldn't." But by that time Martin is already through the door, closing the door behind him, and the lieutenant is beyond reach.

He finds himself confronting the Director of the project, who seems to materialize before him in small bits and pieces of impression, sitting behind a cluttered desk in a near-crouch, his round face, slack in repose, being put together in stages before his very eyes as he responds to Martin.

"All right," the Director says. "There you are after all. I'm sorry I kept you waiting but you can imagine that there were a few things to do here. Have a seat, Martin. I want to talk to you for a little while."

"The launch—"

"The launch. Well, I'm sorry we pulled you off that but there's absolutely nothing to be done, you know. The press can get along quite nicely without your interpretations anyway. Go on," the Director says, "sit down."

Martin sits uneasily, feeling the panels of the chair shift underneath him. He puts himself into a brace to stay unmoving under the Director's eyes. Looking closely at the Director, the weight of his face, the complexity of pain he sees hidden somewhere, he begins to have some comprehension of the lieutenant's occupational problem.

The Director is an ex-politician, or at any rate he is a politician in temporary retirement. Until three years ago he was the Governor of a Midwestern state with serious intentions of campaigning for the presidency, but at the nominating convention he capitulated suddenly to another candidate at the last instant, allowing that candidate to win the nomination and subsequently the election. The Director, at least according to certain newspapers on the scene, had been promised the vice-presidential nomination in return for going over to the other candidate, but shortly after he had done so, a Senator with an even larger bloc of votes had done the same and the Director had been frozen out.

He had similarly been frozen out of various cabinet seats for political reasons having to do with a scandal in his home state during the election. (It involved only the state auditor and treasury department but since he had appointed both there was a certain nominal involvement. Instead, the President had made him the head of this agency after the previous Director had handed in his resignation on the heels of a disaster in orbit which the Director seemed to take more personally than anyone else; he was convinced that the whole thing had been a plot of the engineers, manipulating to embarrass him and get him out of the project.)

For three years, then, the ex-governor has been Director of the project; like most political appointees, he has not expected to have a great deal to do with the actual day-by-day workings but the fact is that he has had a good deal of involvement, even to the point where during the Accident he had come into the communications at a critical point to try to reason with Martin. It is more or less understood around the project that the Director remains ambitious and that he may even move, finally, into a cabinet position if the President is re-elected, but the Director has stated repeatedly that he is linked inextricably to the base and at this time can conceive of no career outside of it. Martin can at least half-believe this and he can believe as well almost all of the conjectures that have come up from time to time during the Director's tenure. That he has enormous influence, that he has no influence, that he is fatally ill, that he is in blooming health, that he is going to sweep the project clean, that he is on the verge of being fired. The point is that no one seems to quite understand the man, while being quite clear as to his consequence. He is not a man to be ignored; unlike most of them, he is felt everywhere.

"Now you listen to me, Colonel," the Director had said to him as he approached the fifth cycle, "I've been following this nonsense and I don't want any more of it. Now you get hold of yourself and do your job. They'll be aborting most of the exploration down there thanks to you and they'll be back in a couple of hours; until that time I want you to do what's necessary and stop this. Be a man."

"You don't understand," Martin said, "you don't know what's happening up here, you come onto that microphone and start giving orders as if they account for something. Now for God's sake, show some mercy and let me alone," and Director or none he had leaned his forehead against the cool damp of metal, sobbing and beginning once again to pray. He had prayed for all of them although the substance of that prayer had not been the normal ritual.

"Don't you see?" he said when the prayer was over. "You can't understand what's going on here. It's immense."

"We know perfectly well what's going on up there, Colonel," the Director said, "but I'm afraid that you're going to have to get a hold of yourself. You're a responsible man, aren't you? You've gone through levels of training more difficult than anything which confronts you there. Now you stop this nonsense or I'll make sure that you're court-martialed and sent to a common stockade, a military prisoner."

"You can't court-martial me. I'll be a hero. I'll be the only man to return safely from a terrible and tragic mission. You couldn't lay a finger on me; I figured the whole thing out."

"You think you're cunning but you're not, Colonel. In fact, you're being very simple-minded for a man of your background. We can do anything to you that we want and get away with it, including locking you up in solitary for fifty years. Now stop dreaming and be responsible."

"I'm not afraid," Martin said, "I'm not afraid of any of you anymore, I've been trained by fear for six years but I can't be intimidated," and that was the last he had had to do with the Director for the time being; there was no way that he could explain to the Director now or then that the reason he had not done what he needed so desperately to do was not concerned with the Director's threats but with something else entirely. Something that he could not quite explain. But then, why should he; why explain? At some point in the recovery, the medical staff had told him that the Director was not mad, understood perfectly what had happened, had sent along best wishes for his recovery and wished that he could spare the time for a visit but could not due to other pressures, would do anything personally within his power to help, and so on. That had been quite enough. He had not looked forward to any further contact.

"As you know," the Director says, looking at Martin abstractedly and then swinging his gaze to the window which gives him a long panorama of the center, the flat buildings, the check points, the gates controlled by guards and dogs, the air now lowering with an obscure pollutant which seems to bring the sky softly and finally closer to the earth, "as you know, Martin, we're going to release you at the conclusion of this mission. That can't be any surprise to you. There were a few things I wanted to discuss in relation to that fact."

"I understood that you would probably release me," Martin says. "I mean, that doesn't surprise me as you say. I think that it's for the best and I've been kind of looking forward to getting out."

"I can imagine. We wanted to retain you for a time for various reasons that you might understand. But it's much better for the agency and for you if you get away soon."

"I think so," Martin says. "I think that you could say that. I have no skills for this job anyway and I detest reporters."

"Don't we all?" the Director says, drumming his fingers on the desk. "Still, I understand that you're not doing too bad a job. Naturally that isn't the point these days, what kind of a job we do; we've had so damned much trouble recently that I think the only press hanging around here now are the bottom of the barrel. Those that the papers can't get rid of all the way. There's going to be an entirely new public relations approach coming up in the near future which may help this problem. I just don't know. Too many details. Too damned many. Are you feeling better? Do you feel recovered?"

"I guess so," Martin says. "I don't think I'll ever be really recovered. I don't think about it too much if I can help it. That seems to be the best way, don't you think?"

"What are your plans? Do you have any plans yet or were you going step by step?"

"I don't know," he says. He realizes that he has never, exactly, thought about this. "I have the pension coming up of course and there are some savings."

"Savings are important. Man like you must have saved quite a bit."

"I guess I'll find a job somewhere, maybe in industry. I haven't thought all this out yet. Of course," Martin says, "my expenses may be somewhat reduced. My wife is going to leave me and she won't be asking for alimony. Isn't that nice of her? So that means I'll probably be able to do very nicely on the pension money for a time anyway."

"I heard about your wife," the Director says flatly. "These things happen."

"Sometimes."

"It's a personal problem; I'm sure that you'll work it out for the best. A lot of the women aren't too happy with the program, as you may know. We should have thought more about the women, because we're picking up a lot of problems now. I don't want to go into specifics, you know, but you have company."

"She always hated it," Martin says. "Even from the beginning, the first days in, she wanted to get out. So it was only a matter of time for this. But she didn't have anything to do with what happened to me. I think that I accept that now. At the start I kind of blamed her a lot but now I don't, not anymore. It was all personal; it all had to do with me."

"It usually does."

"I wanted to say that I'm sorry about those things I said to you from the ship. There wasn't any cause for them."

"Well, that doesn't matter," the Director says. "Don't worry about that at all. We've had so many problems," he says rather vaguely, "problems in a lot of areas. I don't want to go into that now; there's nothing to be resolved."

"I hope I didn't make more."

"A few," the Director says. "Nothing terminal, I promise. That all stayed under wraps better than we might have hoped. That's what I want to talk to you about, part of it anyway."

"You don't have to worry. I wouldn't say anything about it. How would I be in a position to say anything?"

"Oh, I didn't mean that," says the Director, waving a hand rather indolently. He seems, despite his weight and florid complexion, to have been overtaken by a sudden vagueness, a politician's querulousness, that is, something more contrived than otherwise, but on the other hand it is with a genuinely abstracted air that he pulls a cigarette out of a pack, looks at it for a while and then, deciding the other way, crumples it and throws it into the wastebasket.

"I hate these things," he says. "They should go all the way and outlaw them. That's the only protection you can have but the interests, the pressure—you have no *idea* of how they still control things. I try to pace out my smoking, you see: so many in the morning, a couple in the afternoon, the quota system and almost nothing at night, but you're always ahead of quota so what's the sense? You're just kidding yourself; that's my theory. What was I saying?"

"Cigarettes?" says Martin.

"Cigarettes. Oh yes. No, the other thing. We trust your confidence absolutely. No one thinks that you aren't to be trusted. This is highly unusual, incidentally—my seeing you myself. Usually we try to work this kind of interview through channels.

It's a little uncomfortable for me too, believe me. Nothing is easy. Nothing."

"Well, with the launch—"

"The launch has nothing to do with it. That's the tip of the iceberg, as we say. No, there are plenty of things to keep you occupied here; you wouldn't have to launch ships at all to run the base."

"Really?" Martin asks. He feels oddly at ease, a certain disconnection sweeping through. The Director does not seem as self-possessed as he had imagined, not that the issue is self-possession. "If you're busy, if you want me to go—"

"Oh, but that can't be," the Director says. "I haven't even said in the first place what I wanted you here for and in the second, I don't think you understand the situation, the gravity of the situation, I mean to say. I'm going to have a cigarette after all. Will you join me? You're out of the program now; go ahead and smoke."

"I don't do it anymore. They made us quit when we went into training. All the way to the Moon I kept on thinking about cigarettes for a time. But after that the urge went away."

"Oh," the Director says, "oh, that's one way to break the habit. I follow that." He lights a cigarette clumsily, throws the match with a *tic!* into a wastebasket. "Busby took this business with his wife very, very hard, you know," he says. "He's stood up to it very well but there was some question, even at the end, about bumping him off the trip. The little girl would have been a good reason and no one would have said a thing but they finally decided to let him go ahead. I almost took the responsibility myself for bumping him but they wanted to hold back. I really couldn't run this thing myself if I tried, you know. There was a psychosis, you know. Were you aware of that part of the background?"

"His wife? I didn't have much contact with those people at all."

"Well, then maybe you didn't know. Anyway, it looks pretty much as if she committed suicide. She was hospitalized for a time but showed a remission so they discharged her to home care . . . but I guess they weren't careful enough. She did it very quietly, though." The Director giggles somewhat unsteadily and, leaning back on the chair, takes a clumsy puff on the cigarette. It seems strange that a man so dedicated to smoking would do it so amateurishly but Martin has suspended judgments. "She was a considerate sort," the Director says and shakes his head. "Most of the wives try to be, which is why they get so bottled up. I'm going to come to the point; I didn't have you up here to talk about Busby. I'm going to have to make an agreement with you and then have you sign some papers to that effect. This having to do with what happens after your release from the project. I'm going to have to ask that you in no way affiliate yourself with a company or individual or institution which would exploit the fact that you've been part of the program."

"Oh," Martin says. "Oh." He leans back on the chair, hears it creak, rears up again and looks out the window where a number of guards seem to be gathered in casual conversation below, looking and pointing at the sky. It seems that they are discussing the launch; certainly an invasion of the grounds by Communists seems unlikely at this point. Decades ago, maybe. "I haven't even thought of that part of it. My plans are so uncertain."

"A lot of our men find themselves in public relations, travel bureaus, product promotion and so on. Or they tie into large companies where their background has some use. This is reasonable. There's never been any objection to this with the right kind of man; he has a perfect right to do this and there's no reason why they shouldn't see some return from their accomplishments and dedication when they leave us. After all, we're rather ill-paying. For a family man. In relation to the training and the risks. So-called intangibles might take a man up to a certain point here but it can't sustain them forever. And they age fast."

"I didn't even think there was too much of that anymore," Martin says. It is true that at some point in the history of the project there was a good deal of money to be made upon retirement; an astronaut could do product endorsements, public relations, even run for office with some support, but to the best of his knowledge this no longer prevails. There are some three hundred ex-astronauts scattered through the country, mostly the cities, and many more in the project who are due for routine release shortly. Also, although Martin has not studied much of this, he gathers that some of the retirees have had spectacular financial failures, some personally, and some on behalf of the companies who hired them. "Not that I'm really interested, of course."

"Well, you're right, there isn't," the Director says and knocks out the cigarette against the edge of his desk, lets the ashes fall through small plumes of smoke to the floor. "Not like there used to be. On the other hand, there are interesting possibilities still available to many of our men when they leave and there probably will be more as the economy relaxes a trifle. But this is not an economics lesson. I'm afraid that we're going to have to ask you to have nothing to do with any of that. We won't have it, you see."

"Oh."

"We simply can't."

"Why?"

"Well," the Director says, "that should be obvious." He coughs and stands, looks out the window, then backs himself against one of the walls. He is a bigger man than Martin thought, not particularly well-coordinated, a disorderly scholarly abstraction causing him to lurch against the wall as he turns. "Damn it," he says, looking at the sole of a shoe. "These places just aren't constructed for people."

"I still don't think I understand," Martin says, still looking at the guards who are now in a small, confidential cluster, much as if they were exchanging dirty jokes. "I mean, I haven't really given any thought to what I would do when I left. I just accepted the fact that I would phase out soon after this flight and didn't go beyond. Maybe I'll even go into writing, I could do a book. I've been thinking about a book recently, a novel I mean. But I don't see why you want to keep me tightly under wraps this way."

The Director's head twitches in a birdlike manner; his eyes solidify behind his glasses. "Under wraps," he says. "That's precisely the point. You do understand then: you don't need any explanations at all. I had hoped you wouldn't. We can't run any risks. We don't want the possibility—"

"The possibility that what happened to me might get passed out around? If I allowed my background to be used in any way—"

"Something like that," the Director says. "Not exactly. Things are always a little more subtle and complex than you people think because you don't really have subtle or complex minds, but you have the general idea."

"Who's subtle or complex?"

"Colonel, these orders aren't mine in the first place. They come from outside, a good deal outside. The Defense Department, if you must know, but I won't get any closer than that. Of course, if the department has been following your, uh, case, they would have to have complete coverage. We couldn't very well conceal anything; all of our funding comes from there and they maintain a complete monitor. It isn't my idea, didn't originate here, although it's a good one. I won't duck responsibility. I happen to feel that they are right. They, we, simply feel that it would be best, Colonel Martin, if you went entirely into private life, if you took up an entirely new career. If you dropped out of public domain, so to speak. Not that we envision any *trouble*. But it would be just as well, all things considered, it truly would be just as well if you dropped out of the focus of attention."

"I couldn't be any further right now."

"You still don't understand why we put you there, do you?"

"What if I wanted to write books?" Martin says. "I told you, I've been thinking about writing a book. Fiction, just general stuff on what it's like to live at the base, nothing autobiographical at all, just personal stuff and so on. Maybe suspense. It wouldn't touch the other stuff and I'd like to do it."

"No," the Director says. He says it quite loudly, the sound seeming to startle him as much as Martin and he removes his glasses quickly as if to stare farsightedly for the source of this sound, then replaces them and walks behind the desk. "No, that's what I mean. We don't want you writing books, Colonel, we don't want you showing up in costume for any corporation, and we don't want you involved in any way with something that would exploit your background. We can't take the risk."

"Risk? What risk?"

"What risk?" the Director says. "What risk?" He leans back, looks at the ceiling, shakes his head as if there should be a revelation scrawled there but it has been erased while his mind was elsewhere. He returns to a posture of attention, deprived of the writing on the ceiling forever and says, "Risk isn't the word. I don't mean to imply that there's any lack of faith in you. It's just that there are people in the Department of Defense who happen to feel—"

"Certain people in the Department of Defense feel that I might break down in a public way and begin to tell lots of facts and details to the wrong people at the wrong time. Is that right? Or did the doctors tell you something else?"

As if in response, the guards in front of the window now explode into laughter. Martin has the eerie feeling that they are trying to show approval for his speech. They swat one another on the back, fold their extended arms below their waists, do deep knee-bends and reel with hysteria. "What did the doctors tell you?" Martin says. "I'd love to know."

"Nothing," says the Director. "They tell us nothing, Colonel, because there is nothing to tell. We're given to understand by the appropriate staff that you've made a complete recovery and as far as I'm concerned we have a closed incident. But this directive must stand. I'm going to give you some papers already completed and I'd like you to sign them."

"Then what am I supposed to do?" Martin says. The Director leans inside his desk, removes a sheaf of forms, extracts two from the top and places them in front of him. "Precisely how am I supposed to make a living? On an assembly line?"

"Nobody wants you on an assembly line," says the Director. Stop being ridiculous."

"Maybe I should go back to college and get a degree in English literature. If I taught Shakespeare at some cow college, would that be far enough under wraps for you? Or would you rather that I got into the medieval languages for you? Low Latin?"

"Stop it, Colonel," the Director says and shoves the forms across the desk. "You're being a little abusive, frankly. Your manners are not terribly good to tell you the truth and maybe I'm willing to sit for a little of this because the government owes you something and you're understandably agitated, but there are limits to this. Very clear limits. We've had a conversation, I've listened to all your ideas and now our business together has come to an end. You'll sign the forms and be on your way shortly."

"And if I refuse to sign them?"

"You'll sign them," the Director says levelly. "You know perfectly well that we have certain prerogatives ourselves and if necessary we will exercise them."

"Sure you will."

"I think you're getting out of this very well, Martin. I don't think you have any complaints. You've wrecked a mission, destroyed a good deal of our eventual credibility, nearly lost us two good men and given us a lot of problems at the highest levels. A lot of agony has been generated over you, Colonel. Now I'm a little out of patience with this dialogue. I'm a busy man and enough is quite enough, thank you."

"There's nothing wrong with those two good men, is there? They don't even know what happened out there. So don't tell me about losing two good men."

"Just barely," the Director says. "Just barely they don't know what happened. Have you wondered about them once you returned? Has it ever occurred to you to ask where they are?"

"I know they're off the base. I understand that that happened right away. What should I care? It's an agency decision!"

"You wouldn't think about it, would you? That was one of the things they told us, that you could block these men so far from your consciousness that there would almost be no memory. You see, Martin, we know a good deal more about you than you would like thinking."

"You just said—"

"I've got a file on you about a hundred pages thick and I know everything about you I want to know. It's in a fireproof cabinet under lock and it's going to stay there forever. And any time I want it, I can pull it out. What do you care about those two, eh?"

"I care about them!"

"Care, you say. *Care.* There are two highly qualified men somewhere who will have to be released permanently from orbital duty because of you and all that you can say is that you *care.* Don't bother asking where they are; they're well taken care of although not so well taken care of as you. But they can't come back. And neither can you, Martin, not ever."

"Listen," he says, "I'm sorry. I really am. I mean that; I don't know whether you believe me or not. You tell me yourself that you know it wasn't my fault and I thought that everyone understood that. I wouldn't consciously do anything to ever hurt this project. This project is my life; I was here before you were. It's shaped me into itself. I just don't like losing every question of my options—"

"Now you listen to me, you son of a bitch," the Director says and whips off his glasses again, stands, wavering slightly, much less unsteady, however, than the last time he tried this maneuver. "You listen to me. You are going to do exactly what we ask you every step of the way. You are going to cooperate with us and follow our orders and stay in line because you have personally almost destroyed us; singlehandedly you have wrecked us, and we are in no way inclined to take your bullshit anymore. You can count it as sheer luck and hope that we don't put you into an asylum and throw away the key, tell everyone that you had had a little permanent heart attack and left you there to rot. Who thinks about you bastards two days after you're down? You don't think that anyone out there can tell the difference between one and the other, do you? We *made* you. The trouble is that you bastards all get inflated; you think that you're something special and that this project is running for you, that you're heroes. You're nothing, you understand that? We can replace you and we can break you; we can do anything we want. Even when you're doing what you're supposed to you're a dime a dozen and when we get a broken piston like you, Martin, you count for absolutely nothing. Nothing! You don't even exist for me anymore. I've had enough of being reasonable with you. Now you sign that fucking paper or I'll put you under arrest. Military arrest, which means that there will be no bail and no appeal and we may spend three years putting charges together while you sit in a stockade. You're a civilian but we can make damned sure that a little military law applies."

"All right," Martin says, and pulls the forms to him. "All right, I'll sign. I said I'll sign!" He finds a pen in his suit pocket, puts his signature on the bottom of the two forms without bothering to read and passes them back to the Director, who takes and slams them into a desk drawer.

The Director looks at Martin with loathing, the panels of his face now discolored with excitement, his glasses dangling from a hand, flashing light from the ceiling. "Do you want me to tell you what I think of you, Colonel?" the Director says, "because I really would, you know. It would be my pleasure and I want you to know finally where I stand."

"Go on," Martin says, "go on. Tell me. Tell me what you want."

"Yes," the Director says, "yes I will. You're a stupid limited son of a bitch who got in over his head and couldn't handle it. You broke down at the worst possible time and got yourself stitched together again but you are now absolutely worthless. The only thing is that now you think you're thinking when you get snide. Do you know what you're really doing? You're just complaining. You learned about complaint, finally. For the first time, one of you monkeys got himself cracked open and now, while all the poison and stupidity oozes out of you, you stand and watch that dribble and feel horrified . . . and you call that horror *thought*! But you aren't thinking, Martin. Not at all. You're the same stupid bastard you always were, only worse because you don't even work anymore. You have personally lost us a mission, wrecked the future of two good men, put this agency in severe jeopardy and made this latest launch a far more perilous situation than you might even think because a lot of people will be watching us very closely now, people who wouldn't have paid any attention to us at all unless you hadn't screwed up. I have absolutely no use for you and it takes all my restraint not to throw you out physically this minute. I can't even be polite to you anymore. You repel me. You disgust and frighten me. And I hope that what I'm saying to you right now gives you trouble all over again because I will call the wagon personally and haul you into the strait jacket. Am I clear?"

"Yes," Martin says, backing up. "Yes, you are clear. I understand you."

"Have you ever had to set a congressman up with a woman when he visits the base, just to keep him happy? You ever have to do that little job personally and check with the congressman later to see if you appealed to his special tastes? You ever been on that detail?"

"No."

"Well, you've missed a wonderful opportunity. A pity we can't set you up for it. We've had a lot of that kind of duty, recently. I'm very expert at it. After a time, you learn."

"Yeah, I guess you do."

"Perhaps I have caused you to break down again, Colonel? Do you feel that this assault is affecting your mental stability? Tell me. I can stand to hear it, really I can. I want to know."

"Hell no," Martin says, going to the door. "No, I do not feel myself breaking down. As a matter of fact, I think that I'll just get out of this in one piece."

"Not if I can help it."

"Sir," Martin says, "do you know what it's like to be locked up in a training mission? It's not as awful as pimping for congressmen, but think about it. Do you know what it's like to spend six weeks living in a cubicle with two other men, two adult males: the smell of their bodies, their arms and legs sticking into yours all the time? Do you know what it's like in a simular? They pile you into this machine, see, and they put you under ten gravities. Ten gravities is more than you get in the launch but they want you to be on the safe side and really get used to pressure. When you get ten gravities on you, the eyeballs feel like they're imploding, just dropping into the sockets and draining into the mouth cavity. Ten gravities also does interesting things to your balls if you get it three times a week for a month, just to put you in shape. Have you ever tried to fuck after your balls have been slammed that hard? Or do you think that the congressmen have enough trouble getting it up?"

"I hate you, you bastard," the Director says. "I hate everything you stand for. But you aren't going to run out on me, you fucking son of a bitch. Not right away. You're going to stay there and hand out bulletins until touchdown and if you move out before then I'll have you committed. Because I can do it. But if you are seen on these grounds twelve hours after the recovery, I'll have you incarcerated anyway. Do you hear me?"

"You take seven gravities on launch," Martin says. "That isn't as bad but you're only able to be unconscious for so long because you have to make contact just as soon as you hit the stratosphere. You have to sound sane and competent when all you want to do is throw up inside your helmet which would be very messy and dangerous. That can get to you too."

"Get out of here."

"I'm going," Martin says and opens the door, goes out the door and closes it, sees in a quick look over the shoulder of the young lieutenant that the lieutenant is now drawing an intricate picture of the female genital as seen from the point of male entry, shading in all of this carefully with cross-hatches. Small trickles of sweat move over the lieutenant's face; he is concentrating hard. His tongue protrudes over the edges of his teeth.

"They don't look exactly that way," Martin says quietly. "You'd better get yourself some more direct experience. They're a little narrower, at least the ones that I've been working with," and with that he leaves the reception room.

There is a bad instant where he thinks that the door might stick on the exit-line but it gives, all in a tumble it gives and he moves out rapidly, closing the door behind him, trying to force a slam which will not come. All the way out and past the building check point he endeavors to keep his mind perfectly blank; this is what the training advises during moments of stress.

The guards still seem to be exchanging dirty jokes but stop him for a check anyway. "I know a good one," Martin says, when his credentials are restored. The guards give him puzzled looks. "Really," he says, "it's really worth it. Go in and ask that lieutenant what he's sketching. You won't believe it but it's worth the try."

He heads back toward the communications building. The ship should be near orbital fire now and he can favor the press with some of his personal experiences during that time. It is one of those advantages he could lend the job which had been so prominently mentioned in the bulletins that had been released announcing his new position.

XIV

BUTTO BUTTO BUTTON

XV

He does not remember the voyage home too well. Nothing is clear past the—

—BUTTON. The BUTTON is vivid, everything else is muddled. Somehow, he had gotten past the fifth orbit and the men had returned to the ship and from that point everything is blurred, terribly blurred; the retrofire was arranged by one of the others and the passage home to earth indistinguishable from the longer time of catalepsy in the hospital. He remembers—

—leaning against a wall he remembers sobbing, he remembers telling the people of the United States that he cannot stand this anymore, that they have unwittingly created something too monstrously evil for men the damp of the bulkhead—

—he remembers—

—telling one of the others that it was perfectly all right, he didn't care, he could tell them the truth now and the other one, the bastard, had said that there were no transmissions arranged homeward bound, that a harmless breakdown in communications had been announced; he had cursed the man terribly and told him that he had prevented his message, his rare and precious message from reaching the planet which needed it so desperately and needed the truth, but he had been so tired, too tired to move and the others had been watching him closely. He could not get over the feeling even to this moment that the insight he had had on the fifth swing was fine, capsulatory, it would place every-thing that had ever brought them to the Moon in total per-spective and if he could only find the right words it would summarize all of the missions forever but he could not say it, could not bring himself to say the words that would be their doom; he could only convey emotions: sadness mixed with exaltation because at last he was beyond lies and he understood that they had been lying to him about it for a long, long time and now at last there was no need for it anymore. He could meet those lies with truth, the explanations with contempt—

—he remembers—

—voiding thickly within his pants, the urine lying against his flesh like stigmata—

—he remembers—

—despite the insight, despite what it had done for him, how he huddled against the walls of the capsule and remembers begging for forgiveness as the unconsciousness in deceler-ation had swaddled him like death, he was in death, riding death toward the Earth, and when they pulled him out of the sea he was singing.

XVI

When he was young, Martin had read pulp magazines. Western and detective and science fiction he remembers and it was difficult to keep all the stuff from getting mixed up together: range riders and the syndicate, rocketships and powerful blows, alien monsters and stolen horses. The science fiction was what he supposed he had read more of than the other kinds, however: it appealed to him because it simplified things enormously. In the science fiction magazines of that period there had been stories of men who had gone out into the Universe in great rockets to conquer civilizations and make them safe for earth; now and then these men had had problems of course but nothing which the great rockets (to say nothing of a shade of physical violence) could not resolve and the aliens, when they had not been menacing, were usually stupid and in severe need of educational reform.

The stories, then, were full of machinery: there were elaborate descriptions in some of the more inventive stories about how the rockets would be improved and faster-than-light drives and switches into hyperspace and so on and although Martin had not read any of these magazines in twenty-five years, he guessed that there was an admission somewhere on tap here: it kind of stayed with you. It was the kind of thing that would. He couldn't say for a moment that any of this had to do with getting eventually into space himself. Space, for him anyway, came in an entirely different direction and like most of the men who had come in at the same time as he did, more by a series of coincidences than otherwise. But yes, the magazines were interesting.

They were very interesting; no getting away from it. The descriptions of the machinery were fascinating, and the best thing about the stories was that in most of them the machinery was merely something that was used to solve a problem. Men would use the machines to get out of a difficult situation and into an easy one, they would apply themselves to the invention of machine performance and the question was never raised at any point along the line as to whether the machines might create problems of their own simply by being there, or whether a man fooling around with machines during most of his adult life might not be affected in particular ways and might not even risk becoming a bit of a machine, with all the bad and the good that that could entail.

Of course, that might have been stretching the implications of the story pretty far. The magazines were read mostly for entertainment and sometimes they were educational as well. But Martin finds himself wondering these days—ever since the Accident he has been trying to do some thinking, not that he was ever trained to think in the direction he is now trying and it is very difficult and usually frustrating—whether the stories would have been any better if they had indicated that the men dealing with these machines were people too and the situations and complications which came out of this were not to be ignored.

Damn it, something might happen inside a man who was working with machines. Something might even fail to happen inside a man working with machines. This is a tough area: Martin knows that he will not be able to push it very far but it is worth thinking about; exactly how much of the project, as he has come to understand it, has been put together by people who are influenced primarily by the view of the world which was in the pulp stories which he had read when he was twelve years old . . . and whether these people would be in any condition to understand the basic problems if things ever began to go wrong, outside of technical malfunction.

To the extent that he has been able to look at things in this way, Martin suspects that the Director may be one of those people and that what the Director cannot stand is the fact that Martin is not *working* anymore, that he is not performing his tasks in the approved, efficient way . . . but it might be better, perhaps, to try avoiding stereotypy and seeking easy explanations to people like the Director. In the bargain, what has happened with the man, on some level or another, has sickened him sufficiently that he is not sure how objective he wants to be about it. There is still plenty of room for objectivity (a space flight would be a good starting point for it) but this need not be the time.

It worked out better in the magazines, but let's face it, Martin decides, it has worked out pretty well here too. The ships fly, they attain orbits, they land on the Moon, they return. It has worked out better in many ways than anyone would have had a right to expect and what has happened to him is more likely something of a special case; it is not the pattern. He has, since the Accident, been doing research, looked into the background of the project to see if there were any foreshadowing instances, and he sees that there might be certain indications, incidents in the past which might in some way have related to his own disaster, but he does not want to see things too easily or force conclusions where none may exist. For the most part the project has worked very well; most of the mistakes when they came were mechanical and he, Richard Martin, is an isolated instance.

Carpenter. White. He knows this. Carpenter had screamed in the capsule on the seas, begging for release, convinced that they would never come; Carpenter had in fact forced the mission to early conclusion because he could not stand the interior of the capsule. White had panicked at the end of the rope when he had lost the ship and had begun to sob in space. Grissom, at the very end, had said terrible things before the flames knocked out the transmissions. But flames would force curses from anyone.

He has read the transcripts, the confidential and complete transcripts of the agency, on file at the base and now and then his involvement has felt twitches of connection: there seem to have been some precedents. But Carpenter and White had had nothing on him at all. What has happened to Martin is entirely new and there is no getting away from that, no matter how he wants to make the equation.

The ship, the ship in space, takes orbital fire and he feels his own guilt like a rosy glow inflaming his body; as the ship has taken power, so he has become a conductor for culpability and he feels himself burning: burning with a darkening fire whose stain, if it were to surface, would mark him eternally.

XVII

They all have a break after the successful launch from orbit. Until the scheduled telecast, several hours later in the evening, he and the press have nothing to do. The press makes a few desultory queries about his emotions as he saw the Earth dwindle (Perkins seems to be among the absent, only ten or fifteen reporters are there during the maneuver) and he tells them that he felt both bad and good; bad because he wished somehow that he could be with them but good because in the dimunition of the Earth as the rockets fire you can see its beauty receding and know how precious a haven this is in the cosmos. He does not discuss fear, of course. It is a standard response, he may be the fiftieth or sixtieth who has given it, but the press seems pleased. There is no real questioning, however, and the press seems interested in nothing more than a drink and a prepared release. He decides to go home.

He has a right to go home; it is no longer as if he is concerned with this. He goes to his car and drives cautiously out of the base, then takes the Mercury at higher and higher speeds on the highway to their home five miles away. The car roars with power, acceleration, doom; the doctors have told him that he is perfectly free to drive but sometimes, seeing the speedometer nick eighty, he wonders; there is more speed here than in seven miles a second. He clocks the five miles in less than four minutes, pulls into his drive-way, and goes inside to catch his wife in the very act of leaving him.

Several valises are heaped unevenly in the living room; atop the dining table is a neatly-typed note, and Susan, emerging from the kitchen door to look at him with dismay, says, "You weren't supposed to be home until late tonight. Now you told me that."

"I had a few spare hours," Martin says abstractedly and picks up the note. "There was nothing doing so I thought I could come home, might as well. Let me read this thing now."

"You weren't supposed to read that until I was gone!" she says angrily and then her face loses some of its even tone and color and she says, "All right, I was going. I was going; you knew that already. So what? I thought that it would be easier this way."

"Sure."

"I said, I thought it would be easier this way! Don't give me that superior nonsense."

"I just thought I'd read it," he says mildly. "I'd like to know what was on your mind."

She looks very attractive, Susan does. She is wearing a sleeveless, tight sweater of the kind which she so rarely affects these days, and a moderate-length skirt. Obviously these are the parts of a suit which she has not completed and he reflects that in different circumstances, a long time ago, he could be incited to sex just by the sight of her in certain aspects, a tilt of face, flash of upper arm, motion of her hips against a skirt and so on. Not too many years ago they had had a very frequent sexual relationship which he supposed he had made the mistake of equating with quality; still, how the hell could you tell what went on inside their heads? You could only judge by the frequency-content; the other part was insane and obscure.

"Just let me read this note," he says again, "since it was written for me. Then, after I look it over, then I'll talk to you."

She comes over to him, reaches for it but he is cunning, holds it high above his head. "I told you," she said, "I told you, it wasn't meant to be read until I was *gone*, damn it."

"Courage of your convictions, Susan."

"Oh the hell with you," she says. "I'm going to finish dressing. I only wanted it to be easier for you, that's all."

"Easier for me," he says. "That was really very kind of you, very thoughtful." He touches her lightly on the stomach, pushes his wife away. She resists for a moment, then gives ground abruptly and says, "The hell with you," and returns to a kitchen appointment.

He leans a leg on one of the valises and reads the note. It is fairly long, relatively restrained and impeccably written. Susan had minored in English, composition as a matter of fact. It seems, the note points out, that they have reached a point where the inevitable is clear and can no longer be postponed. There is no point to further delays and evasions since everything has really been settled for quite a long time. She has a great deal of feeling for him still which is something that he may not know but that has nothing to do with the real situation which has clarified to the point of becoming unbearable.

She suspects that he has some feeling for her as well and it is for that reason more than any other that they must do this now, make the break: so that they can preserve some small fragment of what they might have had together and remember one another with kindness. Kindness is all that the world has left; it may be all that we can ask of one another; it may save us yet, not that she wants to wax philosophical.

She will not tell him where she is going. It is none of his business, but in the second place, she does not think that he would even care. As she has said before, she will ask for no alimony or support, not ever. All that she wants is an unconditional, uncontested divorce. Whatever happened to him on the flight—and she is still not quite sure of what happened to him because no one really trusted her enough to give her the truth of almost anything—but anyway whatever happened to him on the flight, she wants to make clear to him, has nothing to do with this decision. She would have done it anyway; it was fated to happen.

Long before the flight she had decided that this was the only answer and had known as well that after the flight would be time enough to do it. She could not give him further agony during training and preparation when he would be so occupied with important tasks. She has great sympathy for whatever happened to him but since he will not open himself up to her she can assume that her sympathy is not wanted and that it is not sympathy which he is now seeking from anyone.

If she felt that her staying a while would make things easier for him, she certainly would. There is no cruelty in her; she is not a vicious person. But it is so obvious that they have reached a tacit meeting of the minds on this subject and want the same thing that she need delay no longer. He has made a fine recovery and she has helped him the best she could, in what little way she might, and now she might be entitled to think of herself because self-love is also important if we are ever to have anything to give to others.

There are certain things in this marriage so personal and so precious to her that she knows they are as much a part of her as lips, hair, hands, breasts . . . and these moments will never be known with anyone else, never revealed to a person. They will comfort her for many years to come and enable her always to remember him with love. They had something between them.

She knows he will understand. The lawyer will get in touch and out of his understanding he will cooperate in every way since all of this is really to his advantage. She could cost him a great deal of money which he will never have to spend. She hopes that he will find peace forever and knows that if *she* ever does, a good part of it will have come through him.

She has made a couple of prepared meals for him and left them in the refrigerator. All that he does with them is heat and eat.

"That's a good letter," he says, folding it carefully and putting it in his pocket, noticing that she has been observing him for some undetermined time in the doorway of the kitchen, her suit jacket now in place, her hair freshly in order. "That's fine. That's really fine. You write extraordinarily well. I told you that you had talent for it."

"Stop it."

"No, it's really great. I'm not being sarcastic at all. It really is."

"I didn't mean to write well, Dick. How can you say something like that to me?"

"I only meant to compliment," he says. He takes the letter out, looks at it again. "Listen," he says, "I have a very good idea. Instead of my keeping it, why don't we just turn it over to you now that I've read it? I think that you might very well be able to make some money from it. You could publish this as the confessions of an astronaut's wife in some magazine. They love that in some of those places and it's really handled well."

"Stop it!"

"Oh, I know why you can't. Here: have I guessed it? They have you under wraps too. That was part of the agreement. So you can't publish anything personal for the rest of your life."

"I don't know what you're talking about. And I'm not waiting around to find out because I'm not getting into dialogues, Dick."

"Fine."

"Everything to be said has been said. It was all over with a long time ago and now there's nothing more. There is nothing to say!"

"You know," Martin says quietly, leaning against a wall, hands in his pockets, "that's the second time that I've gone through this today. There was another guy, a couple of hours ago, a guy who said that he had nothing more to say to me and *then* he began to talk. Oh boy, did he have things to say, as it turned out! But you're so beautifully right, Susan. So let's not talk anymore. Okay. You're right. You win everything. Just go. Leave the house."

"I am leaving the house," she says. "I called for the taxi and everything. It'll be here any minute and I'm going then."

"That's very nice," Martin says. "That's fine. That's just the way it's supposed to be done, right? Did you pick that up from one of those ladies' magazines? The whole procedure is beautiful, just like a launch—"

"Dick—"

"It's exactly like a launch, even the countdown is there for the taxi. You pack your bags, you leave me a long letter, you make a couple of meals and you run for the cab. The bags go in the back, just like an orbital, and then you have retrofire. It's really well done, Susan. You have a good sense of style. If only you'd had that kind of style fucking, we might have gotten somewhere with that potential."

"Bastard," she says, adjusting her suit jacket and kicking one of the valises lightly. "You're a bastard. What do you know about fucking?"

"You'd be surprised—"

"What are we *doing*? I don't want to talk to you. I won't even get into this now. You wanted me to leave you. You wanted me to leave you a long time ago. That was all settled, wasn't it? I stayed beyond any point where there was business staying. You haven't wanted me for years. Say it. Know it. This is pointless."

"Sure it is."

"Pointless! And I won't have you getting obscene with me, I won't, you have no right, I never wanted it to be that way." She seems on the verge of crying, then with a shake of the head gives that up. "I won't," she says. "I won't."

"All right, Susan," Martin says. "Your timing is exquisite of course and really appreciated. Of course I'm appreciative; you couldn't have picked a better moment the way things worked out. I guess I'll be too absorbed in my duties, isn't that right, until the return of the ship and by that time they'll have me too occupied in being fired. So nowhere along the line would I have an opportunity to get troublesome. Excellent. You're really good, Susan."

"I won't talk," she says. "Not anymore." She goes to the window, looks out, then comes back to him. "I always hated these houses," she says. "The whole thing was all wrong. The taxi will be here any second and I'm going to go and the rest is for the lawyer. I've got myself a lawyer I can trust and he'll handle everything. Let me leave that way."

"I'm not trying to stop you. Have you seen me once ask you not to go? I'm being very cooperative, you know, and I'm showing a lot of restraint. It's the first time I ever had a wife who left me, you know. But I just want to ask one thing."

"Nothing. No."

"Oh come on, Susan, be sporting. Be as cooperative as I am. Is there another man involved?"

"What are you talking about?"

"I said, 'Is there another man involved?' Simple question, I think."

"No. No there is no one else involved. No one! What do you think—"

"It's funny. We never discussed that side of it; it never came up. It just assumed that we drifted apart like in the ladies' magazines. But I don't know. Is there someone else?"

"How could there be someone else?" she says. "In this miserable place, this miserable life, where the hell could you find anyone if you wanted which I incidentally did not because I never thought that way and anyway could an astronaut have an adulterous wife? That's impossible. No such thing ever happened. Appearances. Keep them happy. Public relations. I tried, Dick, I tried very hard to give you that."

"Because it would be delightful," Martin says, "it would almost be funny if, when you came right down to it, it would be a simple case of adultery and that's all that was ever going on here. Catting around while you talked about emotional complexities. I think I'd pass out laughing, I really would. I mean, I realize all those deep emotional factors that are working here and so on and all of the intricate things between us but frankly I'm sick of deep emotions. Susan, I am a simple man and I want to stay simple if you don't mind. It isn't my fault that I've been thinking so much recently. That's from outside."

"You're raving."

"Huh? Well, anyway, I do think that there's another man involved."

"You're crazy," she says, and closed the suit jacket protectively over her breasts. "That's all, you're crazy if you think that. No, I'm sorry I said that. I shouldn't have said that Dick, and I apologize. I never meant to call you that."

"Don't apologize. Doesn't mean a thing. This is the day for being called crazy. Hell, I *did* flip out, didn't I? Everybody knows that. But let me show you just how crazy I am as long as we're on the subject. Busby."

"Busby?"

"Busby. The guy on the way to the Moon right now. Do you know him? I bet you do. I bet it's Busby you've been fucking."

"I can't stand anymore of this."

"Sure. Why not? He lost his wife a year ago; he probably has normal feelings or he wouldn't've had a wife to begin with. So we know he's not a fag and anyway they never let fags in the space program. No sir, they'd let a Communist in first and let him put the red flag on the Moon."

"Oh God," she says, "I can't take this." Her eyes however do not show fear; there seems to be another quality there altogether. "Too much," she says. "It's too much for me."

"So we know he's not a fag," Martin says again. "He's lost his wife and he's got to pick up where he left off. Who wants to jerk off in his mid-thirties? You can't stay in mourning *too* long; you might forget how to. So he wants to get back into action but there isn't a hell of a lot of opportunity in this place, much less for a man deep into detail for a flight. As a matter of fact, the way things work around here, you're probably the only available piece of meat on the post."

"Am I supposed to take this? I'm supposed to stand here and listen?"

"You're not leaving yet, are you? Busby, now. I bet you've been screwing him for months and months. And now, the day your lover gets shot into orbit—and it was a spectacular one, let me tell you—this is the day that you've decided you can no longer be two-faced. You cannot betray him in this fashion. You must share his danger. You will be loyal and you will leave me, wait for him alone."

"You *are* crazy," she says. "I won't take it back this time. You're a very, very sick man, Dick, if you see things that way."

"Sick. Sick Dick. But I broke down," he says. "Remember? I went clinically insane or at least a little bit psychotic on the flight. Surely you know that much. That wouldn't be any surprise to you. I broke into a lot of little pieces and they patched all of them together again. So here is Martin, the whole man, but things are a little bit crooked: a compulsion there, a little bit of hatred here, over in the far corner an obsession, maybe a fear of animals, get the colors mixed up, afraid of noises in the night, strange feelings about old men, trembling around the lips. They didn't quite patch me together perfect you see but under the circumstances it was a good try. Nobody's perfect. Who's perfect? I'm just a little more off-center than the rest of them. So I broke down and got put together again but I see things different. Not the way normal, sensible people like you do, people who do reasonable things all the time. I say you're fucking Busby."

"No," she says. "No I'm not."

"Sure you are," he says. "Why not?" He thinks of the dreadful economy of it, the wonderful predictability and sense of compression which more than anything else the project gives to its participants, the way things dovetail, the way there are no accidents that cannot be subsumed. It is a new line of thought altogether. Meanwhile, there has been a knocking on the door. Susan runs to open it; he watches her ass waggle, thinking what a fine ass it is; strange that he has not for many years tried to fuck her in the bottom. Hemorrhoids. Anal complaints and he had read somewhere of the possibility of infection. It is a missed opportunity, that is all it is. If she was going to leave him all the time, the least he could have done was to have fucked her in the ass.

A taxi driver stands framed in the door, an average, run of the mill, post-type taxi driver. He holds a clipboard in his left hand, reminding Martin of his own important job. "This the place?" he says.

"Yes," says Susan.

"Oh definitely," Martin says. "You picked exactly the right spot. Exactly. You see, my wife is leaving me."

"Really? Well, that's your problem, friend. I mean, I don't know anything about it. I can't get involved."

"That's a good attitude."

"You work for the base?"

"Kind of. I'm a janitor in the administration building. I swab out the halls after all the administrators have finished straightening things out and go home, leaving their dirt behind them."

"Well," the driver says, "it's not a bad life. It makes a lot of sense. You want me to carry these bags for you, lady?"

"Oh definitely," Martin says.

"You want me to? My back ain't too good, but I can't complain; at least I still got a back. I'll give it a try if you want."

"You want to hear something?" Martin says. "This will kill you. My wife is fucking one of the astronauts. One in the ship out there today. Isn't that the most thrilling thing you ever heard?"

"Wonderful," says the driver. "Just great. Look here, I'm not going to get involved in this. You follow what I'm saying? I'm not concerned with goings-on between the two of you. I got my own troubles; I'm a pretty sick man. You want me for this job or not? If you say no, you still owe me five dollars for coming to make the pick-up. That's an office regulation."

"I want you," Susan says. She has been standing inert through this, her eyes flicking between the two of them, her hands clenched. Otherwise, there has been no indication that what he is saying has had any further effect upon her. "Get those bags out, driver. Get me out of here."

"Ask the man nicely. Don't order him around. Show a little respect."

"I'll handle this my own way or not at all. Now stop it!"

"Stop what?"

"Please," Susan says. "Please get the bags out. I'm sorry. I've got to get out of here."

Mumbling, the driver begins to struggle with the bags, showing a certain low skill; he might have made at least a back-up man on a minor mission. Susan goes to the closet and takes out a coat, shrugs herself into it, staring in the opposite direction.

"How does it feel to be probably the only woman alive who's fucked two astronauts?" Martin asks. "Out of sight, no? What a record. The little lady's going off into orbit."

"You're going to make me hate you very much, Dick. You know that. Is that the way you want me to leave you, hating that way?"

"You, my girl, are fucking Busby. You're fucking him! I can see it in your face. You have a look of far-out distance, lofting, lifting, a yearning, space-borne look. The look of eagles, we here

123

in the project like to call it, the look of eagles as you think of your departed lover."

"I think I do hate you," she says and walks to the door. "Does that make you happy? Now have you got what you wanted?"

"I don't want anything. Not a single thing. I have everything a man could ever want right in this room. How could such a man ever be unfulfilled? Impossible to ask."

The driver returns, gasping, takes the last bag giving Martin a cautious, sidelong look and leaves. "Go on," Martin says. "Get out of here."

She moves to do so, then stops, freezes, turns and confronts him. In some trick of light her face is now strained but younger, tormented but youthful, stricken but empty; he sees some aspect of the girl he leaned over in an old sedan twenty years ago. Her eyes open as if she is confronted by a flower. "What?" she says. "What, Dick? Talk to me."

"I'm suffering, Susan," he says, his voice settling lower through a conscious effort; he will not permit it to break. "I'm suffering. Can't you see that? I'm a dying man."

"I know," she says. "I know that. But I'm not responsible. I'm not responsible for what has happened to you and I won't take it anymore. You did all of this to yourself."

"No. It was the system."

"To yourself. Not the system! You didn't have to live this way. There could have been something entirely different, don't you know that?"

"Maybe," he says, "but maybe not. Maybe it had to be this way all the time and the other part was the lie. Anyway," he says, "anyway, if it had worked out differently, you wouldn't have been fucking Busby. That would have been a lost opportunity. Of course there might have been replacements."

And finally, he receives what he wants. Her blow lands like a caress on the side of his face; it sends small splinters of pain like wine through the cheek, above his eyes, into his head and he reels back, opening up a small space in the doorway. She lowers her head and bulls through that space like a fullback, scurrying as if for cover down the bare walk of their home. "Goodbye!" he says. "Goodbye!"

The driver meets her at the car door, flings it open for her and looking very small she disappears into the back of the taxi like a woman disappearing underwater. The driver moves around to the other side, gets in, closes the door. The cab departs.

Martin stands there for a time. He puts his elbow on the door jamb and watches their path, the cab leaking oil as it proceeds down the street, leaving its own mark of culpability. Long after they are out of sight he thinks that he can smell the fumes, hear the panting of the motor. He stands like stone in the doorway of his house, trying to make some sense of what has happened to him.

But no sense there. Not so simple. So after a time, he leaves the doorway, closes the door, locks it, and takes out the letter. He lies down full-length on the couch to read it again. It is a very well-written document; he is more impressed with it than ever. Not only the language but the implications are now clear. Not only has she been fucking Busby, the letter is telling him, she has loved it.

What the hell has the bastard discovered? How has he made it?

Martin wonders, thinks a little, and eases himself into a light sleep. The sleep will answer some questions for him; surely it will.

It becomes, peculiarly, the first blank sleep that he has had in months, the only one devoid of forms and noises and, unconscious, he plunges into it with an aspect of welcome, feeling disengaged, at least momentarily, from the chains that he customarily carries through slumber. Greeting the unconsciousness like space, he looks around it incuriously, waiting for a sign, if not of invasion, then of malfunction, but there is nothing, nothing waiting for him right now: he can rest.

At the heart of his sleep he connects later with what he learned behind the Moon. It comes to him simple and stark and for the first time can be put into words. Put into words it is not so terrible and he can take it, can even repeat it to himself over and over until it becomes a chant but when he wakes, trying to remember, it is still below discovery. He could have faced it but it will not be recovered. He thinks of the perversity of this.

The rest of the day is still ahead. The telecast from space is scheduled for tonight. His wife's assignment with her lover, carried through fifty thousand miles of ether, darkness, and the whir of machinery.

XVIII

He stays with the press during the telecast.

This seems to be an unstated but necessary part of his job, the standing by through the transmission of public events so that he will be available to monitor, filter and explain. He supposes that things would work out just as well or better without him, and after his interview with the Director he feels little disposed to cooperate further with the project; nevertheless, some strange necessity has driven him from his cot late in the afternoon, set him on his way to the base. Possibly he does not want to face the immediacy of abandonment, and then again, he may be interested in exploring with the press certain aspects of the voyage, which will emerge in the course of the telecast.

Clearly, he does not have to go down to the center to watch things. It is not that important; they can run themselves. Despite the continuing decrease in public interest and despite a real loathing toward the project which he suspects exists in the populace (a loathing which he is sure has nothing whatsoever to do with him; it is just that he is more sensitive to public trends now than he was before he ran into trouble), the networks have still elected to cover the launch, the first telecast from space, the actual landing of Allen and Davis on the Moon and then the descent into the atmosphere. The intermediary telecasts have been scrubbed: no more docking, settling into orbit, views of the Moon or coverage of the antics of the men but the networks have still elected to proceed with three hours of coverage, which is no small investment. The Director might have had to put on heavy pressure for this much coverage but in that respect, at least, he would be valuable.

He doubts, Martin does, if this will continue, the network coverage that is. As circumscribed as he has been within the project, he does not think that there is strong public interest retained in any of the Moon missions. Vaguely, he recalls having discussed something like this with his crewmates on the way to the Moon: in the early hours he had been almost cheerful and after the agony of the g-pressures, companionability, no matter how banal, was a relief.

In order to liven up the telecasts and to keep up the public interest, one of them had suggested that indecent exposure sounded reasonable; one of them, during a transmission, could move in front of the stationary camera to reveal himself bare from the waist down. It would all seem to be perfectly natural, an accident; the man could say that he had been in the process of changing space gear and had momentarily forgotten his state of undress . . . but this single exposure, this one image of a phallus imprinted on a few million home television screens would at the least be sensational. It might even bring public interest all the way back again. Under the context of the voyage, it sounded reasonable.

In any event, they actually got to the point of discussing which one of them should make the exposure. It was not only the size of the penis which was important but its shape and color. Flesh tones would have to reproduce in the most lifelike fashion possible on the new color television equipment they had been provided. Martin, however, had been out of the running from the first. He was childless and one of the men, perhaps cruelly, had said that he could not be a candidate because his working equipment had not yet been proven.

At that point he had retreated from the discussion, rather sullenly, and had eventually ended it by reminding them of the lag. There was a fifteen second lag, they were informed, between the receipt of the telecasts by the network center and that center actually putting the transmission out on the air. During those fifteen seconds, censorship or protective block could be exercised by the skilled technicians who sat in air-conditioned rooms ceaselessly monitoring the telecasts. All that they would get from their audacity, then, would be a canceled telecast ("technical failure" would surely be the excuse) and several years imprisonment back on their home planet to think their sin over at some length. There was nothing to say that control might not even decide that they were expendable right where they floated, these obscene beings, and use the computers to trigger a self-destruct order to the helpless ship.

"They'd rather have us dead than dirty. That's what you're saying," one of the men pointed out and Martin had agreed with the point; that was one of the unfortunate aspects of being in the project. You were warned never to use curse words on a flight because of the possibility of pickup, and to keep your off-duty life as aseptic as possible in order to keep the image of the agency in good working order. You were, in short, an astronaut all the time.

This could, sooner or later, begin to bother a man. At least, it could bother the kind of man (say, a test-pilot) who had taken to casual obscenity without implication as Martin certainly had when he had considered entering the project. (But then, he was not entirely sure; he simply was not quite certain as to what kind of a man he had been when he joined. It had been a long time ago and he had, as they say, been uninformed and not properly indoctrinated into what he would become.)

So, they had given a good clean telecast. They had followed the orders, showing little snapshots of home life aboard the capsule with the shaking out of used clothing and the preparation of foodstuffs and sending their very best to all the families. They had, at that point, behaved perfectly and because of their perfect behavior television ratings had dropped so precipitously that now the transmissions were being phased out. It was more than likely that this telecast upcoming would be the last from the Moon ships in history. Things might pick up again a little when they got into the Mars project in twenty or thirty years (or thirty or ninety at the rate that public opinion was going) but by that time television would probably have been supplanted by something else, maybe direct-consciousness transceivers which would take everybody along inside the astronauts' head for a small fee. The television experience would be irretrievably lost.

Martin decided that he did not mind the probable end of the telecasts. They had been pretty dull no matter which way you cut it and there was no way to really liven them up without going in ways antithetical to the agency itself. He knew what strain they imposed upon the men: the tension, the feeling of observation, the compression intensified by the nervousness of live speech. Control stated that the television screens were rendered inactive except during the transmissions themselves but that was another thing about them which was disturbing. Why should the cameras be controlled sheerly by the astronauts when there was such a lovely opportunity for observation? No chance, oh no chance at all: it is quite possible that the screens are always live and their motions and progress in the spacecraft are being monitored downside at all times. If true this would be terrible . . . but then it would not change things at all except that they might have shut up a little bit. Control itself has shown a certain whimsy now and then although never what you would call a real taste for the scatological.

Martin sits uneasily at the head of the room, by the blank screens, waiting for the telecast to begin. It is scheduled within the next five minutes. Now, he has a peculiar sense of exposure: the press, in its usual mumbling clump, is looking at him as if they somehow felt him to be the producer of the events, the telecast wholly under his control. In addition to that, there seems to be a hint of mockery in their eyes, asperity tainting their voices. Perhaps they know something about him or about the project which he himself has not quite measured although if the press has beaten him to something he is in even more trouble than he figured. The short reporter from the in-depth magazine who asked the questions about fear from Allen and Busby had asked a few questions of Martin himself, yes indeed—Perkins his name was, that was the bastard's name—*Perkins*, comes over to him, carrying a glass of scotch, and says, "This is really something, isn't it? Don't you agree?"

"What now? I don't follow."

"Your job. This job of yours. Having to stand in front of all these hacks here and sell them the mission. I bet you're not too happy. You're the real story here, you know, the real human interest."

"I have no feelings," Martin says. "You know us astronauts, no interiors at all." He tries to turn away. "It's all the same to me whatever happens; now don't make a story of it. There's no story there at all but don't quote me on that either."

"Listen," the reporter says, "listen, man, cool it. Stop talking so much; it's not in character. I've picked up a little unconfirmed report around that you'll be leaving us after this flight. The whole business, everything. Any comment?"

"No comment."

"No comment at all? I'd appreciate it if you whisper something."

"I said no comment."

"It would be very interesting if that unconfirmed were real. Lots of questions. Are there disagreements behind that?"

"I really have no comment," Martin says. "I'm not playing games. I mean that." Perkins's touch has made him shudder; he feels quirks of instability, a literally numbing sensation spreading through the flesh. "My plans are entirely separate from what is going on here."

"Interesting," Perkins says. "Very interesting. I thought you said that your plans weren't connected with anything going on here. That means you diverge from the business, don't you? So the report was correct."

"No comment," Martin says. "I have nothing to say to you."

"I'm an accredited journalist. Want to see my card?"

"Go to hell."

"None of you have anything to say to us. We get lots of facts, data, background sheets, thrust and lift charts but never anything to do with the real stuff. The inside stuff going on. Doesn't all of this make you restless? I'm unalienable, man. There's *nothing* you can say to insult me; it ain't that easy."

"I wouldn't know. I never thought about you personally."

"I understand," Perkins says coyly, leaning his face near Martin's shoulder, "that you might have been in with the old man for a long talk this morning. Was that your resignation being taken, maybe? Or were you getting the big word about something?"

"No comment. No comment."

"The old man's a tough bastard, isn't he? No one gets in there unless they're from Congress or maybe I'm thinking of the joint chiefs. He's big on the joint chiefs. Have promotion word for you, eh?"

"No comment."

"You cats learn to say 'no comment' right well now, don't you? That must be the only piece of nontech language they teach you when they got you locked up in the racks." Perkins tilts his head; now he seems both older and younger, the lines of his face creased by inquiry . . . and by a strange, lurking kind of panic. The panic is interesting but Martin does not want to think about it.

"I understand you got the sack this morning," Perkins says. "That's what I heard very confidentially. A leak from a highly placed source; of course we reporters are dedicated to protecting our news sources. Just call it a trusted and dependable authority for news of this nature in the past."

"No comment," Martin says. "No comment. No comment. Get out of here, will you? Can't you see that I'm busy now?"

"You're not doing busy, you're doing make work," Perkins says. "You have no existence at all anymore. They just give you something to do with your hands." He has become, all in a piece now and finally, the reporter from the dream. "Come clean," the reporter says, "come clean and I'll make it easy for you. Keep on holding back and I'll destroy you."

Martin feels himself trembling. He wants to strike out but does not know with what he could connect and he has an intimation of steel, metal density slapping against his outstretched, flailing palm. "No more," he says, "no more, please. See, I'm appealing to you now; I don't want to discuss this anymore. No more."

"You're killing time," Perkins says. "That's what you're doing, just letting the time pass. But let me tell you something. We got our eye on you. We've got our eye on you, a whole lot of people, and we're going to blow the *roof* off. We're going to take the lid off soon one of these days and show all of the snakes crawling around inside, the pretty, deadly snakes and when we do, when we get around to doing that, you're not going to have any place around anymore. None of you. You'll—"

"No," Martin says. "I can't take this anymore. I really can't." He puts his hands on Perkins and pushes violently. The man retracts, seems to turn slippery underneath him and with an overwhelming impression of physical weakness staggers back. "*There*," Martin says but it is pity coming up in him. "There, so much for you," and feels that he has touched something else like Perkins recently, something that he has lost.

For the first time, the others in the room seem to take some cognizance. They stare, there are dim shouts from the back. Martin feels that he is pinned somewhere in the middle; on the one hand

Perkins's collapse under him, on the other the resistance of the reporters. "Please," he says to the room, "please, someone, get this man away from me. Get him away or I'll throw him out. I mean that. I'll throw him out a window! Get him away from me!"

"All right," an old reporter says wearily, coming over to them, his gray hair wobbling on his scalp, "all right now, kid, leave this man alone," and then there are a number of reporters crying for order and slowly Perkins backs away from Martin, some difficulty in this because Martin, to his surprise, finds himself lunging once again at Perkins, being held off only with some difficulty, and goes back to his seat.

"I'll get you," Perkins says. "That's all. Just remember that. I'm going to get you for this. I've got credentials as valid as any man in this room holds and I don't have to take your bullshit any more. From any of you. None of you!"

"Oh come off it," the old reporter says and the others begin to shout curses, but almost good-humoredly at Perkins. "Fuck you!" they say and, "Blow it out your ass, Perkins," and, "Get yourself a haircut and try being the one on top," and so on, all of this with enormous good humor while Perkins sits sullenly, cracking his knuckles, looking down at the floor. Martin, containing himself, takes his own seat slowly.

He knows now that he is being watched intently. There is a quality of attention in this room which he has never before had from the press and may never have again; casting a quick look at the screens to see that they are still inert, he decides to give in to a new impulse. There is no reason not to; the press, he thinks, will understand, if anyone does.

"I have a brief statement before this telecast," he says, "if any of you want to take it down."

The reporters shuffle their feet, look at him blankly. A few remove pens, the majority shrug. "I don't think that this will be on video pickup so I guess you could call it a press exclusive,"

Martin says. "That would be a nice change for you boys, wouldn't it?" There is a slight riffle of interest, nothing substantial but the reporters raise their heads, most of them, and look at him.

"I want to announce," he says, standing and holding the table, "I want to announce my resignation from this position effective with the successful landing and recovery of the mission. That resignation is irrevocable and I want to say that I've had a good deal of satisfaction in working with all of you. It's been interesting and I only hope that I've been informative and reasonably useful. From my side of the table I've found it an education; my business was not too high on contact with many opposing and inquiring points of view and so I think that I am really the privileged one in this relationship."

There is a short pause. Martin perceives in a stunning, sickening burst of insight as he stands that the reporters have nothing whatsoever to say to him and that they are not clear exactly what he has in mind. There are several coughs, a more extended pause. He looks at the floor and begins to think of leaving the room, his shoulders heave, he wonders if after all the events of the day this is the one that will touch him over the line. He sincerely hopes not; there would be no dignity in it.

Finally a reporter says, "Do you have any plans? What do you look forward to doing in the future? Specifics? Industry?"

"I don't know," Martin says, seizing upon the question, resolved to follow it wherever he can. "Maybe industry as you say. Maybe some consultative position. Engineering would have to be considered, aeronautics engineering of course, although my technical background is a little sketchier than I would like to admit. Maybe some goodwill position in which I will be able to work on the agency's behalf to show our young people what the agency is doing which has direct application to their lives. That would be nice to do, now our nation's young people—"

"Were you fired, Martin?" Perkins, maddening, irrepressible, says from a seated position. Others close around him, block him off from sight. "Come on, man, answer the question, get on the ball, show a little life and talk to the point. Were you fired?"

"No comment."

"Bullshit!" says Perkins and the others murmur something around him. "Bullshit! You won't ever speak the truth. Tell it or don't tell it but get off the pot, Martin. It isn't working anymore."

Martin sees that indeed he is in hot water, that he has, as a matter of fact, made a fool of himself; by trying to save a situation he has gotten in deeper—but it was necessary for him to announce a resignation at just that moment and he could not delay it past the telecast; some small, undiscovered piece of himself could only be recovered in that way, he had thought—but it is too late for any of this right now, that part is all gone. It will not return again.

The screens go on.

They whirl with color, a crackle of audio sneaking in under, and Martin knows that there is no getting around it: the telecast from space has begun. "If there are anymore questions, then," he says quickly, "if any of you want to ask me something legitimate I'll be available afterwards but not for very long."

He hopes that this will get a laugh but it does not. Instead his familiar cries, "No one cares, Martin, no one cares. Can't you see that already? No one cares anymore about this," but fortunately he does not have to answer this or deal with it in any way because the sound comes on all the way.

It comes on shockingly high, roaring with information and the spirit of flight and batters the room mercilessly until someone finally makes an adjustment; then it goes to the merely agonizing. Martin sits heavily, awkwardly, balancing his clipboard once again and looks at the screens with the rest of them. He will, after all, have some interpretations to offer afterwards; perhaps he can tell them again about his own experiences in space so that they will be able to understand exactly what it means to make a telecast.

Do they realize that they have simulators and drills for this too? he wonders. The broadcast, rather uncaring, begins.

XIX

A voice-over (for, concede it, it must be admitted that by this time the telecasts are a very slick production; of course professionals have been in on the technical and advisory parts of it from the beginning) says that America is now taken to the voyage toward the Moon and without further transition the inside of the main capsule comes on hard against the camera. The fuzziness and slow-motion of the earliest broadcasts have long since been corrected; the background and the handling of the images is tight and controlled. The camera has been set against the wall opposing the main porthole so there is a fine view of the Moon coming up in the distance. The camera focuses on the Moon for just long enough and is then dropped by the man operating it to the interior itself.

Allen and Davis are sitting in an awkward posture, side by side, grinning at the camera. Below camera range their hands are performing certain gestures; the barely revealed wrists bounce. Busby, who obviously operated the camera, comes into the picture and sits behind the other two and Allen says, a little bit portentously, "Good evening, my fellow Americans. Welcome to our home. It will be our home for seven days less two and a very comfortable craft it is.

"We are now speeding toward the Moon at constant acceleration of something over seven thousand feet a second. We have passed the one-third mark of the voyage and, as you might suspect, matters aboard the ship have already settled into a routine. The *Anna Christie* must be our home away from home; we must try to make it comfortable."

"Exactly," Davis says and nods vigorously, bouncing a little bit in the weightless environment from the gesture. He looks astonished, runs a hand through his hair. Busby gives him a long, sidelong look which is difficult to decipher from the placement of the camera.

"We live," Allen says, "we live very much as you do on a slightly larger celestial body called the Earth, although more narrowly. We wash, cook, eat, work, engage in recreation and socialize although not quite as conveniently and with somewhat restricted options. Let me introduce the crew to you. The man who has just taken a seat on my right is Colonel Joseph Busby, the commander of the command ship during our stay on the Moon and our chief engineer. The man on the left is Lieutenant Colonel William Davis, my partner on the impending exploration of the Moon. We've been in flight for eight hours."

Allen pauses, shakes his head, looks to the right and left of him and says, finally, "Colonel Davis, would you, uh, have a few words at this point?"

This is one of the problems with the telecasts, which seems insoluble. Despite the technical advances, despite the color transmission and despite the really superb ability of the camera to provide a portrait as informal and lifelike as from any metropolitan studio, the telecasts themselves remain stilted, amateurish, posturing. They remain on the level of family home movies and no one yet seems to know quite what to do with them.

Martin recalls that the training process, when it would come to the issue of the telecasts (which it often would) would enter an awkward period. The advisor would tell them, amidst unwieldy pauses, merely to look straight into the camera and remain as dignified as possible. "No one here wants or expects you to be show business stars," he had said, but Martin was not quite sure of this. In flight, atop their obscure speculations, they had some-times had serious discussions of what might be done to give these telecasts a more spontaneous and natural air. Their ideas ranged from singing to an exchange of reminiscences and attitudes toward the flight, a panel discussion so to speak where each of the men could come across to the audience as a person. But nothing had really come of this.

Similarly, there seems to be little going on here; it is strange that men a third of the way to the Moon can find little more to do than to simulate the actions of dimly-recollected family movies but that seems to be the case. Fortunately the telecasts are being dropped; it seems to be the only solution.

"Well," Davis is saying, "not really. I don't have too much to say. It's quite an experience, this. Going back the second time is just as thrilling as the first because you tend to forget the vast-ness, the unimaginable power and beauty of space and to come back to it is to come as if for the first, uh, time. It isn't dark, it's an unnatural blinding *blue*—"

"What are your thoughts as a sociologist?" Allen asks. He does not seem to have forgotten the press conference (not that he can be blamed for this), but more significantly he has the uneasy air of a master of ceremonies who has discovered that the show is running off schedule and that several of the scheduled acts have been reshuffled without his knowledge. "Colonel Davis," he tells the camera, "is a sociologist, of course, the first member of the so-called soft sciences to have been on a Moon expedition. It must be quite a fascinating thing for you—"

"I have no real thoughts," Davis says. "It would be hard to pigeonhole this as sociological, that as astronomical and so on. It's still too overwhelming an experience at this point to order neatly. As you can imagine, one can hardly reach reasoned con-clusions so easily as you might think—"

"Well then," Busby says, "if that's the case then I have a few comments. Colonel Davis seems a bit vague; perhaps I can do better." He leans forward toward the camera, clasps his hands together. His eyes seem to glare unnaturally although this may merely be a trick of the camera; Busby is an intense fellow.

Martin stares with interest at the man who has been fucking his wife. It is useful to see Busby in this newer context; it gives him an entirely different perspective. Busby is the kind of man, he knows, who despite the superficial control and rigidity would probably scream helplessly at the moment of ejaculation, and he wonders if Busby is conscious of this weakness himself or whether he copulates in a void, must be reminded of it by his partner now and then so that she (or he) does not run the continued risk of serious ear injury.

"I have a few comments," Busby says, "you see, we have to get this show on the *road*, that's all that there is to it. Now there are a few details on this which I haven't made clear enough yet and they should be informed, must keep busby, busy, busy."

"Colonel Busby, as I say, is responsible for the manning of the control capsule while Colonel Davis and I are on the surface of the Moon," Allen says. "It's a highly responsible job, probably the key to the mission, and very capable he is too." He gives Busby a sidelong glance; maybe there is a shade of unease there but maybe not. "What hasn't been made clear yet?" he asks, a vague tentativeness in his tone. "Go ahead."

"Why the whole *point* of it isn't clear," Busby says, leaning forward, gesticulating toward the camera, "the whole meaning and the message and the background. Here we are, eighty thousand miles out toward heaven and no one has yet tried to talk about the very serious Implications of this. Theologically and otherwise."

"I thought," Allen says, "that we would try to take you through a typical day on the *Anna Christie*, our craft, and show you how our lives are conducted here. Beginning with the end of the two-man sleep shift, let us pretend that it is 0800 hours. Now, at that time, we would—"

"Hold on for a moment," Busby says, and interposes his body between Allen and the camera. "Why are you playing pretend? Isn't there enough reality here for you? Now just hold on for one little minute, man, because you haven't let me talk yet."

"The Commander is saying something," Davis points out, putting a hand on Busby's wrist. "In a few minutes we'll be able to add—"

"Now cut that out. Just *wait* a minute," Busby says, his voice dodging up an octave or so. "This is definitely not *fair*. This Commander of ours is just monopolizing everything and then I'm not given a chance to answer a question after you've had your say. Who is he censoring? There has to be a little bit of reality here and we have to understand what is going on eighty thousand miles from home. Eighty-two thousand miles by now, I should think. You talked about our constant acceleration. The Commander is a terrific talker, isn't he?"

"Son of a bitch," one of the reporters murmurs in the darkness. Martin, leaning forward intently, chin on hand to better observe the telecast, feels the words hitting him like a whip against his absorptive box. "Shut up," he says. "Cut it out!" The reporter mutters something else, quiets.

"Constant acceleration," Busby says, leaning into the camera so that his body takes up the whole of the line of sight. "Isn't that interesting for a sociologist to think about? It's like the population explosion only simpler, and less fun."

"Why don't we just let the Commander talk," Davis says quietly. Apparently he puts a hand on Busby. Busby's form recedes slightly and then dwindles to a quarter of the screen as he sits.

"I don't know," Busby says. "This doesn't seem very fair to me. Everybody should be allowed to have their say without interruption."

"Now, listen," Allen says, "describing a typical day aboard the *Anna Christie*, we would begin with the preparation of the breakfast foods. For breakfast we would take a packet—"

"Hey man," Busby says with a stunning casualness, "hey there. I got a question I want to ask before you get into this."

"I don't understand," Allen says, freezing, caught in mid-gesture like a man assaulted. "Why won't you let me proceed?"

"Come on," Davis says. "I really think that we should listen to the Commander." His head bobs; a sheen seems to move contrawise to his forehead. Transmission is excellent. "Everything in its turn—"

"Colonel Busby might be a little excited," Allen says, gesturing toward the camera, the sickening smile on his face an apparent attempt at ingratiation. "As we know he is the only first-timer among us, his first time in deep space that is, and it is an experience which could awe any man. This excitement is so natural. I remember on my own first trip, not too many years ago, how I would—"

"Now, I don't want no reminiscences," Busby says, slapping his hands on his knees, turning to face Allen. "None of that stuff, we're way out, about eighty-two thousand miles out protected by only a few inches of steel and this is no time for babble. It is time for men to get serious and talk about basic things because who knows whether and in what form we might return. Straight thinking is the rule of the day! What I want to know about this schedule here, all the way out, is whether there have been any provisions for sex. Have there? I hope that it's in the agenda somewhere."

There is a dead pause. The three men look at one another, Busby no less astonished than Davis or Allen, as if the words had been said by an intruder. *The fifteen second lag*, Martin finds himself thinking, that fifteen second lag, what the hell happened to it? He wonders if the engineers are stunned. Frighteningly, the other possibility occurs to him . . . that the fifteen second lag was something that was created by the training staff to stave off the possibility of trouble they might have seen and that there was never any control exercised over these broadcasts. They could have said anything at all. Nothing was there to stop them.

"What the hell is going on?" someone says in the room. "I don't understand this; it's not the usual stuff. What are they doing there? Do they think that this is the way to get an audience?"

"Sex?" Allen is repeating. "*Sex*?" His face is drawn, heightened, bloodless; it seems to have been pursed into a querulousness teetering on rage but not energetic enough to dive into it. This seems to be the essential Allen, coming out at last through all the wiring and intermediary devices. "I don't think that I understand you at all, Colonel, and I don't think I want to."

"Joe," Davis says hastily, "Joe, I think it would be better for all concerned if you relaxed for a little while. Colonel Busby is a little excited, isn't he?" Davis says desperately, looking at the camera, trying to moderate between the need to deal with Busby and his own astonishment. He is exactly like an actor caught in mid-speech when flames appear under the proscenium: do you finish the damned speech or quash the flames? Or run? "Maybe we'd better put this off until a later time," Davis says. "Joe is a little bit upset, we can see that and—"

"No sir," Busby says and stands. Weightlessness vaults him a few feet into the air. He waves his arms and settles slowly. "No, I'm not at all upset. In fact, I'm in perfect shape. I've been certified by this agency as one of the hundred most fit men in America, I've passed every psychological test known to man and a few that haven't been discovered yet and all I want to do is raise a few questions on this public broadcast so that we can try to get some answers. I might as well get a few answers, don't you think? What's the point? You can't avoid this kind of stuff forever, might as well let a qualified man get into it if anyone does."

"I think that we ought to call this off," Allen says. Sex seems to have utterly fragmented him; he seems older, the querulousness in his voice now plaintive, the voice of a senescent man. "Maybe a little bit later, we can get into a schedule and then—"

"You aren't calling off nothing. You son of a bitch, you ain't calling off *nothing,*" Busby says. He puts his arms around Davis from the rear, hooks his hands into the man's stomach and slowly draws Davis back against him, pressing body to body in a parody of intercourse.

"You're a big man, sociologist," Busby says. "You're Just two hundred pounds of warm, clinging weight. Not that you'd better get any ideas about me from that, I swing the straight way like any spaceman. No, don't cut this off! Nobody down there cut this off or there'll be big trouble. I want to finish my conversation. Now you listen to me, Commander. I'm trying, still, to get an answer. What I want to know—"

Allen says, "I don't think you understand, Colonel. This is a telecast. We're on television. There may be a hundred million people watching this. Now it's funny up to a point but then it stops being funny and I have to insist—"

"Now you listen to me, Commander," Busby says with a horrid casualness. "I've been listening to them for long enough. Now it's going the other way. How much listening can a man take without speaking back? I'm going to ask some questions and I may never get another chance. No, don't even think of cutting me off down there; you leave those circuits open! You freeze me out and I'll break the sociologist's neck."

He seems to put some pressure against Davis, moves a hand up the rib cage to graze the man's chin, place it in a new, less comfortable position. Davis stiffens, grunts, begins to flail like an infant, but Busby holds him steady, only a subtle tension in the wrists indicating that pressure is going on. He has been well trained.

"Now look," Allen says. He reaches toward them and the three mass briefly, gather into a clump, merge into a larger creature. Allen strikes, Busby reacts. Davis kicks, they begin to drift upward.

Weightlessness becomes apparent. The recent ships have been taking a slow spin which restricts some of its effects and along with a certain restraint in motion can disguise it on the broadcasts but now it is all arms and legs, broken rhythms, like the early days. The men struggle, they part from the floor like an unfaithful wife parting from her conscience and begin moving upward, upward in relation to the aspect of the capsule anyway, moving with a cartoonlike complexity toward the ceiling.

Hey! one of the clump shouts and they tense against one another. The pickup is momentarily cut off, total gray as someone floats before it and then the picture returns. Allen in a panic disengages himself from the two of them and floats over to the side of the capsule, bumps into a bulkhead and then drifts slowly to the floor, crosslegged. On the floor he bumps, tailor-fashion, settles, moves as if to rise and then seems to change his mind, shakes his head, gestures.

"Stop that," he says. "That's an order, right now! Stop it!"

"But I'm not doing anything!" Davis says in a high voice, a very high, childish, unDavislike voice, still clamped in Busby's arms. Busby relaxes his grip slightly, uses his feet to find some purchase against a wall and slowly edges back to the floor, still carrying the sociologist, cradling him.

"Let me go," Davis says. "Please let me go. What are you doing?"

"I'm going to take you somewhere," Busby says. "That's what I'm going to do." They land on the floor with an unsettling bump clearly heard on the pickup. Davis makes retching noises, tries again to disengage himself, fails, stops struggling, leaning his head toward the floor. Busby keeps a firm hold on him, leaning toward the camera as Davis thrashes.

"Disgraceful performance," he says. "Show a little control, Colonel, it isn't that bad. As I was saying—"

"Please," Davis says. "Come on now," but he breaks off into spasms of coughing. "I mean—"

"Are we still on?" Busby says. "I wonder. Or did they cut us off. They better not have. I don't think that they would."

"I don't know," Allen says. He looks toward what would be the indicator light which is off the screen's line of vision. "The light's still on for one thing. I think we're still on. What are you doing to us, Busby? Haven't you had enough?"

"Can all the bullshit," Busby says. "It's too late for that."

"It's never too late."

"Oh yes it is. Of course we're still on, I should have known that. They wouldn't have the guts to cut us off. No sir. Not when they're finally getting a little reality. How about some reality, friends? Hey you technicians, aren't you pleased? Finally you're getting a little honest event out of space, none of that situation-comedy garbage. You wouldn't cut us off, would you? I know that those booths down there are just full of guys who have been waiting and hoping and dreaming *for years* that something like this would finally happen. Stay with it, guys. Hang loose. The place is full of saboteurs; you're giving us full coverage."

"Please, Joe," Davis says. "Enough is enough. Stop it—"

"It is not enough, you stupid bastard," Busby says and yanks the sociologist's head back like a ventriloquist's doll, forces the man into an agonized grimace, then skillfully restrains him from struggle. "I haven't even begun to get at the truth of it yet. The fact is that I've had enough of you, Davis: I'm fed up with your sanctimonious bullshit and as far as you, Commander, you don't even know what's going on. You're just barely alive, man, you haven't been with it for so long that you've forgotten. You're a man in a daze, you're staggering through the engine rooms of the heart but none of the machines are working and you can't even read the instructions. There's nothing inside you, Allen. It all went a long time ago—they did it, they drained you dry and you too you pseudo-scientific son of a bitch but they haven't done it to me. Not to me! I'm alive, I'm still functioning. I may be the only living being in space right now and what do you think of that? How would that be? You two aren't alive, you're machines, creations, robots from the agency and I'm the person! You like that, pal, huh?" he says, giving Davis's trapped head a heavy yank. "What do you think of that?"

"Ah," Davis says, "uh."

"Talk, you idiot."

"I have no thoughts. Nothing at all." He seems to have relaxed fully into Busby's grip; there is even a kind of stateliness to his submission. "I don't think you understand," he says, wrenching his head. "You must stop this." He starts to retch again; Busby holds and regards him lovingly, like a mother cradling a petulant child. At length the spasms cease and Davis subsides further into the grasp; he seems to be less of himself every instant.

"Stop it?" Busby says. "Never. You see, folks, I haven't even started yet. There's got to be a real start."

Somewhere to his rear he takes a piece of cloth, tosses it at the camera. The cloth mounts huge in the camera's focus, then falls over it in such a way as to blank the line of sight.

Now Martin can see nothing. The dim whiteness of the cloth shows only faint translucence, an impression of vague figures struggling, darting movement. For the first time since the beginning of the telecast, his attention lapses somewhat: he becomes conscious of what is going on around him.

There are shouts around him, there are noises, the sound of feet hitting the floor, the bellowing of reporters as they seem to shout questions. "I don't believe it," someone is saying over and again, "I don't believe it, I don't believe it," and someone else is laughing (this must be Perkins) in short scatter-gun bursts and many of the reporters seem to be in motion but at the dead-center of all of this, at the absolute middle, there is an enormous stillness; it is a pool of astonishment so large that it makes all of the shouting merely a set of disorganized sounds on the fringes.

And it is into this confusion that Martin vaults as he staggers to his feet. "Stop it!" he shouts, "now stop it! This press conference is over!" and then realizes how foolish this sounds because this is not a press conference but a transmission. Maybe there was going to be a press conference afterwards, surely, that would have been policy, and there he would have given his reflections on the reactions of the astronauts but how can he cancel things out now?

"Stop it," he says anyway, "please, no more!" not knowing if he is referring to the shouting or the existence of the reporters or whether he is indeed talking about the cloth on the camera which blocks their vision. If he could only see what is going on there might be some way of dealing with it but the cloth covers everything; they are utterly broken off from the ship.

He feels suspended, out of touch with the environment, nothing like it since the ship. What he wants to do is say something to this room of reporters which will pull what has happened into a perspective so forceful that they will ask no questions and the event will be closed forever . . . but he cannot. There really is very little, after all, that the agency or its representative could say at this time. The agency, at least momentarily, seems to be without a position, due to the breakdown in scheduling.

The sounds in the room increase. Martin senses panic. What has happened here is totally out of the program: in none of the schedule sheets and anticipated progress reports which the agency has prepared for his handout since weeks before the launch has the possibility of anything like this been denoted. If it had been—if locked neatly into the schedule for 8:00 P.M., September 3, had appeared the note JOSEPH BUSBY WILL

NOW HAVE SOME WORDS ABOUT HIS NEW ATTITUDES WHILE HE ASSAULTS COLONEL DAVIS AND INSULTS COMMANDER ALLEN—if they had done that, perhaps everything would have been all right. It would have shown the agency's rigor and willingness to go out of the routine program, that would be all, and there would have been no problems in coming to terms with it—although the reporters would have grumbled; it made dictating their stories difficult—but just as shocking as what has been going on, at least to Martin, is the fact that *the agency has not provided for it* and there is no way of dealing with it. None at all. There is no precedent.

Even with the history of malfunction on some previous flights, order had quickly emerged and a revised survival schedule had been instituted. Had damaged craft missed the atmosphere and plunged into the sun or skipped into the atmosphere to burn, it would have happened at a predetermined time and could have been fitted into the overall picture of the launch. But this is a new one. Martin is at a loss but harder for him than that is that the agency is at a loss.

And beyond that is something else as well which may be the most serious of all; remember that the rest could be sorted out sometime but one thing cannot be and that is the feeling of satisfaction which has arched through him while watching the telecast . . . and the worst part of it, he has been, in essence, sympathizing with Busby and urging him forward. His astonishment he can deal with but the other is not so sure. It is very difficult. It means, among other things, that the medical staff has not quite been doing the job which they said they did but it dives into areas even deeper than that, into areas which Martin had never even acknowledged until the business with the Director this afternoon. And then his wife. What the hell? he thinks. Has losing her unbalanced him that much? Was she that good a fuck? He knows that she and Busby have been lovers, no doubt about it. He waves his arms again and after all of this, still calls for an end to the conference.

But there is a good deal more to come. There always is. Perkins (it was Perkins who was laughing) has again modulated his voice and is asking Martin what he thinks of this, whether he approves of what is happening. Perkins is ecstatic and wants to know whether Martin has any comment on the overall significance of this latest happening to the development of the space program. Not for nothing has Perkins maintained the attitude of disaster for a long time; he seems to be the only man in the room in control of the situation and himself. "Come on," he says, "tell me, who did the interiors on this one? Just lovely! Would you care to let us know who wrote the script now or should we wait to find out how it all finishes?"

"Someday," Martin says, "someday I'll tell you what is going on." (It had been his intention to say something really devastating, something to put Perkins in his place forever but there is no way around it; he does not know what to say.) "Just you wait," he says helplessly, "just you wait, you wait to see this," and in the meantime, on the screen, the whiteness collapses, saving him from further comment. "I'm waiting," Perkins calls to him, "believe me, Colonel, I'll be waiting." Martin guesses he will be. Although he does not want to admit this to anyone, even himself, he has gained some respect for Perkins within the last half hour. The man has been on to something. He has very definitely been on to something.

Once again the interior of the ship is on the screens, Busby sits before the camera, his face bloated by some freak of enlargement, his eyes wide and bland, his hands twitching slightly. He moves to one side with a showman's flourish, ducking out of the picture—

—Behind him, Davis is lying on the floor, his body twisted into a horrendous position, his face and legs touching. Allen cowers at one corner of the capsule, looking at his hands which he holds before him. "Don't," Allen is saying in a high peep. "Joe, for God's sake, please don't—"

"Welcome again," Busby says in a monotone, "to our show from space. Thank you for bearing with us during our brief time of technical difficulty. We are proceeding toward the Moon. All is well for those of us who remain. As the more alert of you may have observed, Colonel Davis is no longer with us."

"No," Allen says, "please, no."

"The Greek chorus is being brought to you by Commander Allen. Colonel Davis is dead. He is dead due to a certain circulatory failure induced by unknown or perhaps known causes."

"Oh God," Allen says. "Oh God."

"That will get you nowhere," Busby says almost cheerfully. "Not under these circumstances, I'm sorry to say. Commander Allen, bringing you the Greek chorus, may be observed chanting in the background. He seems to fear a similar circulatory failure as well."

"Oh help me. Help me."

"Are you listening to me, Kit? Are you out there? Have you heard me?"

"Please," Allen says. His clothes seem to be twisted out of all perspective, his face has collapsed. "For the love of God, no more. I can't take it. I admit it. I can't deal with it. I cannot control any of this. Please stop it."

"I'm sorry, Kit," Busby says. "You're the only one I'm sorry for but I mean that. It's the truth. I had to do it, Kit; maybe someday when you're older you'll understand why this happened and then again maybe you won't but there's no point in worrying about that sort of thing now, is there? That's all in the future."

Busby runs a hand through his hair, staggers to a standing posture and moves before the corpse of Davis, addressing the camera directly, with a horrid intimacy. "Forgive me, Kit," he says, "I had to do it. I had no choice. There was nothing else for me to do, not a single thing. I know you'll understand that.

"Now you listen to me, you sons of bitches," Busby says and backs away from the camera, lurches toward a wall, then spins from the wall and advances again, slowly, filling the frame chest-to-eyes, a hand drawn into the angle making threatening gestures, "you listen to me down there all of you because this is your last chance. There's not going to be any rerun on this one even if you play the tapes over and over again. This is the only thing that you're going to *get*. I did it and I'm glad. I fucked up your broadcasts and your Moon voyage and everything and I'm happy that I did it. Do you know why? Do you want to know why? How much of this do you think a man can take? That's why. What do you think you're sending, robots out here? Machines? Like hell you are; you're sending people and there are limits, there simply are limits to what a man can take.

"I tell you," Busby says, his voice quavering and then settling into a maniacal flatness, terrible control, absolute precision, "I tell you, I've had enough of this. You took me away from my daughter. You couldn't care less about that but she could have died, Kit, maybe and for all you cared; she could have died but you weren't going to let that change your plans now, were you? Oh no, the flight was scheduled and I was the module commander and that was enough for you. You had a contract! So you locked me up, kept me caged like an animal and threw me into space, but you just can't *do* this kind of thing to people. Kit, Kit, do you hear me now? Do you understand me? Look what I'm going to do to them, Kit, because of what they did to you. I'm going to destroy them. I'm going to get even with all of you for what I did. That was what you were always very big on wasn't it, Kit, getting even, giving back what you got, showing them that they couldn't push you around; well, it gets more difficult as you get older but sometimes you can still do it if you're willing to pay the price and I am, I am. I'm going to fix them, Kit. It may be method, but there's madness here. Method in the madness, madness in the method. Who knows? Do you know what I'm going to do to you, you sons of bitches?"

Allen staggers again into camera range, cowering below Busby's neck. He is comic relief, that is all he is. "For the love of God, Joe," he says in his old man's voice, "please, no more, now stop it," and Busby, with an easy backhand, sends the clown spiraling weightlessly and gracelessly from the picture, sending a clown-squeal behind him. "Oh, Joe, what *are* you doing?" the clown cries and thumps, out of range, against one of the walls, drifts back into the picture like an errant conscience, mouth dilated, finger gesturing, and then is hidden behind Busby's frame.

"He doesn't matter," Busby says. "He's no fun at all, he's agency down to the core, devices and nothing inside him. Do you know what I'm going to do? I want to stick to the point. I really want you to think about this now, I want you to kind of run it through your minds, your hundred million minds, over and over again, give it some real thought because I want you to understand how I've planned for you. I think about you all the time, you know that? I'm consumed by the need to service you. I'm going to show you that you can't get away with this, that there's finally a kind of reckoning and that you're going to pay. All of you. The agency for the agency's sake and the rest of you because you tolerated it and would not do anything to change it."

"The armaments," Martin says in a flat dull voice. He is once again looking intently at the screen; the connection between Busby and himself now seems absolute. They could be discussing things calmly with one another, face to face, two drinks lying untouched between them on the table. "I would have thought of that myself if I had had the opportunity."

"This ship is loaded with nuclear devices," Busby says to Martin. "We were supposed to try some seismic experiments, remember?"

"Sure," Martin says. "Sure. I would have thought of that right away."

"We were going to test the gravitational and quake stresses on the Moon, see how it took some fission."

"Absolutely," Martin says. "I wonder if they ever really had the Moon on their minds at all."

"Well, we'll try a little seismology, you see," Busby says, leaning confidentially toward Martin, "but we're going to try it where it can do some real good; none of this bullshit about experimentation. What right do we have to blast the Moon, eh? We've ruined our own planet, do we have to take it out a quarter of a million miles toward Heaven now? Is that the kind of creature we've become? I hope not. I have a better idea."

"Of course," Martin says. "I wouldn't have missed it, though. I bet I would have seen it faster than you. I had more background."

"Just wait until this ship comes around the Moon," Busby says, waggling a finger archly at the camera. "It flips around the Moon and starts home by itself you know; that's part of the wonders of physics. I don't have to do a thing. Just wait until I come back to you. I'll show you a little fission. I'll come home with a bang."

"Joe," Allen says yet again, crawling back into camera range, his motions in weightlessness like a baby dumped into a tub, "Joe, I've decided to give you an order. That's the only thing to do. I'm ordering you on behalf of the agency—"

"You're finished, you old bastard," Busby says. "You don't even matter to me any more. You hardly exist." He reaches inside his informal, space-traveling garments, removes a knife (now where has he gotten a knife?) and shows it to the Commander.

"You see this?" he says. "I planned to use it on the sociologist but I didn't even have to; he was no fun. No resistance. But I won't be denied—I'll use it on *you*. Perfect element for a spacecraft, you can't use a gun you know because you wouldn't want to leave any of those dangerous holes in the hull."

"Oh no," Allen says and dives out of sight. "Not that. Not that."

"Well, there, ladies and gentlemen," Busby says, replacing the knife somewhere underneath his arm. He gives the camera an enormous wink. "Well there it is. Now you have it. That is the conclusion of the *Anna Christie* show for this evening. I do hope that you've all enjoyed it and that you'll be back with us soon. If you're lucky, and if you hurry back, you may catch the show again on your favorite networks quite shortly. But right now the cast is tired and must sign off. What remains of the cast, that is. This is an action-adventure show." He reaches an arm toward the camera, smiles with contentment as he finds a switch. "Goodnight now," he says. "You've been a great audience I am sure. We'll be back on the air shortly and try to show our appreciation."

The picture collapses, dwindling in upon itself like a smashed balloon. There is a momentary silence in the room, then the noise begins again, a high, frantic noise: screams, mutters, laughter, the sound of many feet hitting the floor.

Martin stands and finds that Perkins is at his side. The man has dropped his pad, his glasses, his manner and is standing erect, arm at sides, trembling. His breath seems uneven.

"Well, Colonel," he says, "what do you think of your mechanical men now? Tell me, are you going to be able to cover this one up too? What are your plans? What part of the schedule was this one on? The revised schedule I mean to say. What basic geological and industrial research has been accomplished here? Tell me of all the benefits of this flight to the millions of starving and dispossessed citizens of America."

Martin levels a cheap shot. It is about time; there is an enormous sense of release to it. He unloads a left hook which catches Perkins on the jaw and knocks him, clattering and moaning, into a pile of reporters in front of him. Perkins falls straight down, hits the floor hard, begins to convulse. His arms and legs twitch like those of an insect impaled on a pin. He begins to drool, cough, cry.

Martin emits one shriek—oh God, oh God, he has been saving this shriek for such a long time, he is entitled, finally, to get it out—and hurtles from the room at full speed. The reporters part for him, their eyes opening with fear. Maybe they think he is Busby. Maybe he *is* Busby. This would be no more unlikely than any other things happening today. Perkins could be an epileptic; this would be very unfortunate.

Martin runs: he runs through all of the corridors with equal ease—nothing appears to be manned anyway—and comes to his car; he drives out of the area at insane speed, accelerating, finally, on the flat, dead road, to over a hundred miles an hour. The owner's manual hints that it can take a hundred and thirty-five but it is beginning to gasp and pull at a hundred and five and that is probably an exaggeration on the speedometer. Junk: it is all junk.

The engine gasps, stammering for a lower gear but he forces it grimly to the last possibility of speed holding it in fourth, hands clamped to the wheel, looking over the dark, empty spaces of the new South at night. He thinks of nothing whatsoever and somewhere midway in the drive for reasons which he will never comprehend he—

—recovers some sense of himself; for the first time in over four months he connects with the man inside and although he is a changed creature, this interior self, he guesses he can bear it. At least he knows what he is now; he knows too what he has become.

He slows the car. He rolls to the side of the road. He sits inside the parked car for a time shaking his head and keeping his hands on the seat, pressed flat into the upholstery. Then, finally, he makes a U-turn and heads back toward the project.

The flat land seems open to doom. In swiftly lowering fog he thinks he can see the network of fire which the bomb will lay down . . . and himself at the center of the fire, ascendant.

XX

"Now," they told him after the fourth orbit, "do you hear us? We're going to get them back right now. We're going to abort this mission and bring them back to the capsule right away. They are firing off the Moon within the next ten minutes. They will be back in three hours. Do you read us? Do you follow? Do you understand? Will you hold out?"

Would he hold out? By that time he had been babbling, babbling and singing: rational conversation, back-and-forth, stimulus and response, struck him as having nothing to do with whatever was going on inside of him and the business with the Director had just about finished it off; if this was the head of the agency and this was the best that he could do, the furthest that he could go with one of the astronauts, then there was no point in pretending toward rationality anymore. It was all out of control. The BUTTON had told him that a long time ago, and finally he was listening.

"I read," he said, "I read you, but why should I? Why should I hold out?" and he winked once again at the BUTTON, the lovely inert BUTTON that never spoke to him on the earthside swings because they understood one another too well but became articulate during darkside and once again told him the secrets. "Why should I?" he said again to the BUTTON and nodded at his friend, "after all, the whole thing was to make a mark on the Moon, wasn't it? So what better tribute than to leave the two of them down there?" Oh boy! the thing had been terribly clear to him, absolutely central and beyond doubt was this sense of clarity which he had reached; he was able to understand now not only what was going on but the hidden meanings, the actual purposes. "We want to leave ourselves on the Moon, don't we? That was the purpose of the whole thing. Hell, we've left flags and memorials and tablets and pieces of underwear and shoes. Why not put the real article down there?

"Anyway," he said, raising an eyebrow at the BUTTON, "I'm getting a little restless. I think that it's time for a little retro-fire." He leaned toward the BUTTON, which they caught on the visuals, and this drove them absolutely insane and they began to plead with him, telling him of the disgrace, the eternal disgrace of what would happen to him if he abandoned these men, the scar and stain which he would carry for the rest of his life and besides that the mission had great scientific value. It was all for science. He didn't want to be the man responsible for the aban-donment of the whole project under a tide of public revulsion, did he? How could he do that just when the time of the real breakthrough was on hand? Hell, if they were able to get down to the Moon three or four or five more times there was no saying what they might pick up. They might even have a theory for the origin of the universe. And the public was counting on him too, the faithful, innocent public that depended upon its heroes and would not be able to understand what had happened if he let them down. The public had paid for the project; they were enti-tled to heroes. How could Martin not understand that?

"What the hell do I care for the public?" Martin said. "The pub-lic doesn't care about any of this, don't you see? They don't give a shit. All that they're conditioned to understand is that this is a *show* and we've been giving them a good time here. It's about time that they understood what was really going on here though, don't you think? They don't give a damn for us anyway. I'm going to get out of here. They hate me; I can feel their hatred penetrating a quarter of a million miles. Don't you think that they hate you too? Wise up, men, it's bread and circus time again."

Control had raved, control had preached, control had ranted and threatened and pleaded and cajoled; they had advised and stated and warned but control was having no effect upon him whatsoever. Not anymore. He had put up with that shit long enough, now he was his own man, the hell with control. They were just a goddamned group of technicians in trembling fear of politics was all they were and even the jokes they made were invariably lousy. There they were, hundreds of loveless men in a room in the southwest, using their voyeur's equipment to poke and pry into his capsule. They knew his heartbeat and kidney function, they had his bowels wired and his urinary tract, they knew his sweat content and the reactions of his stomach, he was wired up like a carburetor, but there was one thing that they hadn't wired him up for yet (although they surely would have liked to try), they did not know what was going on in his head and he had his head left. And so, the hell with them.

The hell with them! Their goddamned machinery and equipment and eternal orders and adjustments, well they had a surprise or two coming to them and no doubt about it, they were going to learn what kind of man they had here. He would show them. He did not give a damn; he had his own problems and considerations and, besides, the BUTTON and he would settle this once and for all on the fifth go-round and then he would press the BUTTON, on the darkside, let them sweat out this one and think they were getting through to him and the two of them would head back for Earth and a generation of peace and celebration. Because his coming home would end the war too, he could bet on that. The war was all tied in with the project; the one made possible the other and if the project collapsed they could no longer cover up the war. They would have to send the war to the Moon and keep the project under wraps on Earth, that would be the only answer. So they would win two ways, not that he had ever had much of a position on the war until now; it was just one of those things, like climate, that you just learned to put up with. When you came right down to it though it wouldn't be a bad thing to get rid of the war too. He supposed that he would just as soon.

"Listen," control said, trying a new tack, "listen to us, you can't do it, you'd only fall into the sun anyway. That's the way it works. You don't know how to make the adjustments on your own to save yourself.

Martin thought of fire, the lovely, lovely fire arching through and around him as he drove himself through the arc of the corona, how the flames would embrace him and carry him to their core like a lover, and he began to laugh anyway. "I don't care. Don't you understand that, you sons of bitches?" he said. "I just don't care anymore; I'm not on Earth, I'm nowhere within your cycle and you can't get at me. There isn't a single thing you can do to me and I am a man without fear. Fear won't work anymore, it can only go so far but then no further and I'm out of it, out, you hear me?" as the ship moved steadily toward darkside.

Darkside: darkside reaching toward, enveloping him and he had risen to greet this darkness, all the solutions enfolded him and he knew that he was free. Free once again, just him and the BUTTON, it had been so clear on the fourth orbit around that the end was near.

There was just no way of anticipating what was going to happen to him on that fifth orbit. Maybe it had been a fool's paradise not knowing but it had been nice anyway; a pity that it could not last. He knew that they deserved it down there. He was giving them surely what they had always wanted, all the blank men with headphones sitting at their desks, staring at the screens. They had taken degrees and fucked joylessly and bought houses and gone into debt for possessions just so that they could be ready for what he had to give them. At night they dreamed it, it would appear to them in the cover of dreams, this end, and now it was coming closer and closer: he would give it to them. He would give them a disaster so enormous and irrevocable that they could only give up and join with it forever. They would no longer have to cope, they could let everything go in the simultaneity of collapse. Oh, they had had a taste of it, a little foreknowledge with the Grissom fire and a good hint with the White business and then the Carpenter (Get me *out* of here! Get me out of *here*!) and the business with Thirteen in its calculated, beautiful stupidity had brought them even a little bit closer but they were still not quite ready for it. They insisted upon struggling against their destiny, they had not yet learned to accept it, they were still trying to act as if their headphones and desks were real and as if they were in a rational business. But it was not, it was not rational at all—

—there was nothing sane about it. How clearly he saw it! How clearly they would see it. Darkside took him beckoning and in darkside a kind of apotheosis. How could he know what was going to happen to him then? But he had tried, Richard Martin had tried and in the attempt had come closer to it than anyone ever had before. Of that he was sure and as far as the rest of it, the hell with them. They would have to sketch out their own salvation against the Dome.

Just before he slipped in all the way control said, "Your wife, we have your wife here. Talk to your wife, quickly, before it's too late," and Susan, helplessly, began to say something but they had fucked their timing, fucked it good and proper like everything else and before he could hear her words he slapped into the clouds of the Moon and heard no more. Her voice cut off in the middle of a prayer, eternal isolation, like the cloak which dropped over him when he finished fucking her and fell heavily to one side, already moved toward catalepsy, toward disconnection.

A quarter of a million miles of technology to find the same blankness, the same pain.

XXI

It is ten o'clock when he returns to the base. He hears this on the car radio, which has been playing, all over the dial, old music and local format programs. There seems to be no mention of the telecast although now and then an announcer will say something about standing by. The mindless rhythms of the music entice him, he bounces in the seat, hums along with the choruses as he pulls the car into the base. The lights are on throughout the area: harsh as day and the checkpoints seem to be manned by double teams. As he takes the car to the gate he finds himself surrounded by guards who wink in the dazzle of the strobes, appear to move erratically in the throes of some exhaustion. Their uniforms are crumpled, their eyes refract pain. *We the living—*

"I don't think anyone's allowed in," says one of them after he shows his identification. "We have a general order to keep the base sealed off. Maybe you should go home."

"That won't help," Martin says. "Besides, I've got to be in there; I've got an important job. Couldn't get along without me."

The guards consult among one another, backing off a few paces. "Listen here," Martin says, "don't you think it's a little too late in the day to be procedural? That won't go any more; it's a whole new era and anyway. The press will be very anxious to see me." Sometime toward the end of the drive he has been formulating the outlines of a statement he will make to the press. Surely by now everyone in the world will know what has happened (and has anything happened since then?) but he has gotten the idea that a few words from him are desperately wanted by the press so that he can give them the true, final explanation of what has occurred. Who is better qualified to do this? "I don't know," one of the guards says. "I guess we should call the Director."

"Now listen here—"

"We have to. If you want to get in it's highly irregular, we have to find out what he has to say. If you want to leave, you can."

The Director has played no part in his imagined schedule of events; he has, in fact, completely forgotten the man but now he is slammed against it. "Okay," Martin says, "all right. Go on. Call him. He'll want to know where I was anyway. We have a very close relationship, the two of us. We understand one another."

The guard nods, pouts, picks up one of the mounted phones and talks into it quietly. He stands for a while, shrugs, seems to get another line, says something again and then nods. "All right," the guard says. "You can drive in there."

"I thought so."

"The Director wants to see you immediately. There are orders that you be escorted directly to his office right away."

"But you see I don't want to see him."

"Those are the orders."

"I have nothing to do with him anymore. I'm pleased by his interest, of course."

"Look friend, I don't know anything about you or about what's going on," the guard says. "This isn't my affair. The word is that you're to be given an escort there and I am to be that escort. Move over in the car, I'll drive it."

"The transmission isn't too good. These Mercuries don't hold up at all; the thing doesn't kick down to lower gear on acceleration."

"Oh, for Christ's sake, take it to a mechanic," the guard says. "Take your troubles there. It isn't my department." The others seem to draw into a pack, muttering; the guard opens the door, pushes Martin skillfully into a corner and gets behind the wheel.

"I don't understand nothing," the guard says. "I just don't know how you people work anymore, how you think, and I never did." He puts the car into gear, cautiously, and they begin to inch forward. The guard regards the road with interest, jiggles the gas pedal, perhaps looking for a downshift.

Martin, jammed against the door on his right, thinks for a moment of jumping, realizes exactly how far that would get him and decides to stay in place. Maybe the Director has an apology to make. That is not impossible; the man, in light of ensuing events, now feels guilty over what he has said and wants to make amends with Martin. Not that Martin will ever accept the apology; the Director and he are quits. Then again, maybe the Director does not want to apologize. He is a prideful man and what has happened may simply embitter. Whichever, there is nothing that he can do about it except anticipate, which would only give the Director satisfaction. "Has anything else happened?" he asks.

"Happened? Where?"

"On the flight."

"I haven't heard a thing, champ. I don't know what's going on. I've been on the patrol here since nine o'clock this evening. They ordered up some extras and I got the call."

"Why the extras?"

"Who knows?"

"Didn't you watch the telecast?"

"What telecast? I don't think you understand me at all."

"The transmission from space."

"Oh."

"There was a transmission from space this evening. Didn't you see it?"

"I don't know anything about it. I don't watch them anymore; they're pretty boring. I tell you, I don't follow this stuff at all. I'm a civilian. I don't have any connection with it."

"Then you don't know what happened?"

"What happened?"

"You don't know."

"Oh boy," the guard says. "I told you, I got no interest. No interest in this stuff. If they didn't make the noise today I wouldn't even know they had a takeoff." The guard leans over, winks at him. "Tell me, did something happen? Is there some stink? Is that the reason they called up the extras?"

"Forget it," Martin says and restores himself, reluctantly, to a posture of attention in the car, looking around him, trying to get the general picture. The base, at least from this vantage point and at this hour, seems normal—that is the interesting thing. It has the desultory nighttime look of an out of the way airport. For all the effect that the telecast has had upon the normal life of the base, it might as well not have happened at all or been a bathroom dispute between the three men occurring in a roadhouse several miles down.

Most of the buildings are dark. A few have lights within them but they are the standard, night maintenance fluorescence, nothing exceptional there. The press building has a good deal of activity around it but the press building is always active for reasons he has never quite understood. Only the administration building which they now approach seems to be altered. It is surrounded by guards and guards, hundreds of them, standing only feet apart, arms folded in a line, looking toward the sky. A number of reporters seem to be making desultory attempts to break the line and get into the building. Inside, every light is on. Martin shrugs as the car stops and gets out before it has even come to a full halt. "All right," he says, "I'll make it from here."

"No you won't," the guard says. "I'll take you up there. That's my orders and I've got to do it. It's nothing personal."

"Martin," another guard says, breaking from the line and coming over to them, peering through the strobes. "Yeah, that's who it is all right. Come on," he says, snatching him by the arm. "Now we got to make a little run. Let's get a move on. No stalling, man, just *sprint.*"

It is too fast, too fast to think. Held in tow, the guard's damp hand hard on his wrist, Martin breaks into an awkward run, then, as they approach the line of reporters, lowers his head and in time with the guard begins a full charge. He has not exerted himself so much since the re-entry. Looking at the scattering faces of the reporters, falling before them he begins to have some sense of impact, some intimation of what effect the telecast may have had (it was hard to believe in the car that it had had any effect at all). The faces of the reporters are stiff, frantic and they grab at him, touching his shoulders as he and the guard dodge through the line.

"Martin, Martin, what the hell is going on?" someone calls and several others begin to shout for a statement. "Statement!" they say, "we have a right to know" and so on and the guard gives him a warning pinch indicating that he should say nothing. Of course he will say nothing. What is there to say? What do they want to hear? But their shouting has some aspect of attack, of violation and it goads him into something close to fear. He and the guard pick up their pace and burst through the line, take the outside steps three at a time at a full run. He feels an ominous rattling in his chest that could be pistons gone awry; he has never been conscious until now of heart action.

"Son of a bitch," the guard says at the top of the stairs, grasping his own chest and running his hand rapidly in that area. "My God, I can't take this anymore, they're going crazy down there," and his breath ragged, moaning, he pulls Martin into the building itself.

Inside, the quality of light is abnormal. Every bulb, every strobe, every hidden piece of fluorescence in the place seems to be on and the halls are filled with noise, movement, worse than outside. Personnel seem to be shuttling through the hallways constantly and doors down the halls slam rapidly, aimlessly, disgorging new people in streams but all of the people seem to look the same. Some of them appear to recognize Martin and stare at him with inscrutable expressions which more than anything else mirror the gaze of the reporters. The building rumbles.

"Going crazy," the guard says, "going crazy," and tugs him into an open elevator. The operator on this usually unmanned car moves switches and they ascend rapidly, the operator looking at his reflection in the small mirror to his right.

"What's going on?" Martin says, "tell me, what's going on in here."

"What the hell do you think is going on?" the guard says. "Don't ask me; I'm not talking. Ask your questions inside. They always had the answers there."

The doors of the elevator open, they stagger into yet another hall, pass several more guards and go into the reception office of the Director. It has changed from this afternoon, seems smaller, tighter, not fully shielded from the noise which comes from below. "That's it," the guard says to the familiar lieutenant who is standing by the desk, one arm slack, looking at certain papers scattered over the top, "it's not my responsibility anymore, I got him in here. Don't say I didn't do it now, here he is, I'll testify to it," the guard says and, without looking at Martin again, leaves. Martin wants to touch him, explore the possibility of a relationship but the guard is already out the door.

Panting from the run, disoriented from the transition, he takes a seat, rubbing his hands against one another. He tries once again to blank his mind, a habit which has been partially successful for a long time although in recent weeks it has been running thin.

"You," the lieutenant says, perching across the desk, "you, Martin, where the hell have you been?"

"Why? What's the difference?"

"You ran out on us, Martin," the lieutenant says. "At least you made a good try up to the last minute. Well, so much for that," he says and presses the intercom, says something into a receiver, replaces the receiver and looks at Martin with an expression of loathing more intense than any he has seen so far. "All right," he says, "they want to see you. Get your ass in there."

"Who is they?"

"Some people. Never mind. Tell me, Martin, were you seriously expecting to get away with it? You really thought running would work? I'd like to get some insight into your mind. What did you expect you'd accomplish?"

"Listen, you can't blame me for what happened. I didn't do it."

"You don't even know what's going on, Martin. You're out of touch."

"I didn't mean to run. I thought that I was free to leave if I wanted. What's the difference? What role do I play in this?"

"I'll tell you something someday, Martin. I'll make the whole thing clear to you. I'm waiting for that day, believe me."

"Me too," says Martin. "I'm fed up, do you hear me? I am not responsible for everything that goes on here. I'm not responsible for even a fraction of it and if you hassle me anymore I'm going to belt you one. I may be out of shape but I have a little condition left." He walks through the doors into the Director's office, leaving the lieutenant to think about this. He doubts that the lieutenant will think very much.

In the office, the Director, more disarrayed than he was even at the conclusion of their interview, sits uneasily, cross-legged at his desk. In front of him is a full cup of coffee in which a cigarette butt floats like a dead insect. To his right is a short, nervous man with bright eyes who looks at Martin with quick interest on the entrance before turning away, turning to look out the window toward the open spaces of the center. Illuminated in the light, they seem brighter than they do by day. Martin can see the line of guards outside, the leaping reporters and several trucks of communications equipment from the networks which seems to have just come in. The Director looks at the trucks, shakes his head and rolls down the shade. "Sons of bitches," he says, "now we're really in for it. Now we'll get it. Here comes the equipment."

"So they'll sit," the short man says. "What the hell's the difference? They're not going to get anything, they might as well be there as anywhere."

"Where were you, Martin?" the Director asks. "You made yourself unavailable very quick. We wanted to see you immediately. We've been waiting several hours for you by now."

"I went for a drive."

"That wasn't very responsible of you, was it? What made you decide to take the air at that particular time? Had any ideas?"

"What the hell was I supposed to do? There wasn't a thing."

"Yes," the short man says, slamming a hand on his knee, "that sounds like a reasonable statement. What was the man supposed to do?"

"What's, uhm, happened?" Martin asks. The question seems pointless; he has asked it merely for the situation's sake. "Anything new?"

"My name is Oakes," the short man says. "John Oakes. I've come here to talk to you, Martin, as well as a few other people."

"Oakes is from the administration," the Director says almost obsequiously. "He's pretty highly-placed. You'd better listen to him."

"Don't overdo it," says Oakes.

"I'd like to know what happened," Martin says again, "if anyone will tell me."

"You mean you've been out of touch?" says the Director. "You didn't even put on your car radio. We're expected to believe that?" He stands, an odd weariness causing his joints to sag under pressure rather than stiffen, and walks to the window shaking his head.

"I put it on. They didn't say much."

"They couldn't say much. We don't know what's happening. There's no transmission. He knocked off the equipment for us."

"Can't you pick up the capsule anyway? I thought you had a camera sealed in there always operational."

"Yeah," the Director says, "that's right. But there's an override on it and he found it."

"That's interesting," Martin says. "We used to talk about it now and then. We always felt that there would be something like that in the cabin so that you could maintain surveillance. But we never thought there would be a way to cut it off."

"There has to be. For security reasons, in case of invasion or so on, so that the enemy could not have access to the capsule. There must be that protection."

"That's fine," Martin says. "We worried about enemy invasion all the time."

"Well, you can't take chances," the Director says rather vaguely. "You know how it is."

"Sure," says Martin. "I'm sure that it was the right thing to do. But anyway, there's an override."

"The capsule is due in Moon orbit in about two hours, Oakes says. "If there's no correction, it will turn around and head back by morning. So there isn't much time you see, Martin, and I've got to talk to you."

"I thought we were talking right now," Martin says. Somehow it is difficult to take much of this seriously: the two men, the disarrayed office, the question of the capsule. More than anything else, it seems historical, a collection of artifacts and fossils which represent events of a long time ago. He feels his reality oozing away from him as he stands there.

"You know," he says mildly, "it's all your damned fault, you understand. The whole thing. You have no one to blame but yourselves for this."

"I don't understand you at all, Martin," the Director says. "But then I guess I never did." He gives Oakes an uneasy stare, mumbles something, sits again. "I told you there would be no help here," he says. "We settled all that before."

"I suppose that what with the telecast you've got yourself a pretty good panic going on out there. Am I right?"

"No," Oakes says, "you are wrong. Not that I blame you for the mistake. You got the full pickup in the information room but actually the networks knocked it off after he covered the camera the first time. Which was pretty alert of them, we think. We're pretty grateful."

"I guess you are."

"Of course," Oakes says delicately, "there have been a lot of inquiries. Some people tend to question the broadcast."

"I guess you talk about technical malfailure, huh? Malfunction, is that the way to put it? I'll verify that to the press if you want."

"Not exactly," says Oakes. He takes out a handkerchief, considers it for a while and then blows his nose vigorously in a sound that comes over a little like a sob, then folds the handkerchief neatly and repockets it. "Sinuses," he says. "Probably tensional in origin. I think that the problem is a little bit beyond the solution which you advise. We've discussed it, of course, but it isn't quite satisfactory, I'm afraid."

"Don't you understand we're wasting time?" the Director says. "This whole goddamned thing is a waste of time. Stop jollying him! Get to the point."

"Just hold on," Oakes says quietly. "Let me pick the spots here. This is my problem, not yours." He looks at Martin intently. "And your problem too," he says. "We need you, you know. We really need you a great deal."

"Is that so?" Martin says. He leans back, trying in the face of the situation to remain relaxed which, under these circumstances, is surprisingly easy. He finds that he can do it, that he can even feel to some extent on the offensive.

It is not a confrontation, for one thing (these people seem to be beyond confrontation), and for another he thinks that he might understand Oakes well. He may have misjudged the man—people in the project have made a career of misreading people from the "administration"—but there is a strong impression of lapsed control in this room. The Director seems to be little more than a witness which is nice and then too, Martin cannot get over the feeling that Oakes understands more of the situation than even Martin does . . . and Martin feels that he understands the situation about as well as anyone could; with only a little difficulty he could have written it. In fact, driving on the desert, he had had the feeling at one point that he had done exactly that, that everything was somehow an extension of his own desire, that all of this had been staged and programmed in his own mind. "So they're asking questions," he says.

"No," Oakes says. "That's the interesting thing about all this. There's surprisingly little concern. Of course, it would be impossible to pick up the whole of a national reaction from one desk but everyone seems to be very calm. No unrest at all. Of course, we're getting a lot of phone calls, mostly from people who want to know how it all came out. They seem to think that it was part of the production plan.

"You see," Oakes says, and takes out his handkerchief again, "you see, as far as I can deduce anyway, these things were so devalued a long time ago that they're just another kind of television. People don't believe what they see on television anymore so this becomes part of the general mix. It's very hard to get people really involved these days. They've seen so much. And television, I'm sorry to say, is a very poor medium for what we like to think of as reality."

"I know what you mean," Martin says. "I did some thinking about that part. I really know what you're saying."

"We suspected you would. I didn't have any doubt that you would get the point."

"But you like it, don't you, Martin?" the Director says. "It gives you a great deal of pleasure now, doesn't it? You look to me like a man in no distress at all. I knew that it would give you pleasure. You don't have to conceal your feelings; put them right on the table. This is the best thing that has happened to you in four months, isn't it?"

"Just wait a minute, John," Oakes says with a wonderful, expansive, soothing gesture. "Just hold on. It isn't the time for analysis yet. This is just between the Colonel and myself at the moment."

"You couldn't be more pleased, could you, Martin?" the Director says, but without passion. He is already withdrawing, shrinking into a corner of his chair. "Why, you probably feel like a whole man again."

But Oakes is right. The dialogue is obviously between the two of them; the Director has no further role. Martin, in that knowledge, feels his mind making vaulting leaps, swooping connections, power oozing through him. Oakes and he understand one another. There is no need for these two friends to go at things painfully, they can get to the center of the matter. "Why don't you knock him out of trajectory?" he says. "Can't you trigger the automatics by remote?"

Oakes leans back, looks at Martin with thin approbation, runs a hand through his hair. "That's pretty sharp," he says. "I told you that this was a bright man, John. Your perspective is altogether narrow if you won't admit to that now."

"Why should I admit to anything? Find out for yourself. That's what you want, isn't it? He isn't that bright," the Director says with a deprecatory gesture. "His intelligence quotient tested out at 112. But he's cunning, I'll give him that. All of them are cunning. Underneath that exterior, they're as sly as they come.

Of course they can get too clever for their own good as this one did and then the cunning doesn't help at all."

"We can't do that," Oakes says, turning back toward Martin. "The trajectory business, I mean . . . that would have been our first thought, of course. But there's got to be a safety factor on that one too, an override in the craft in case of computer failure here or there so that you don't get an abort or worse on the mission. The triggering can't be remote; there's got to be a confirm at the other end. Otherwise you get dysfunction. So," Oakes says again, "there's an override switch." A strange appeal drifts in and then disappears from his eyes. "He's turned it on, you know. That would be the first thing that he would think of, don't you suspect? This man isn't stupid; he wouldn't have gotten this far if he was."

"Have you been in further contact with him?"

"I said he's knocked off the visuals. Audio pickup we do retain. That he can't override. It's a safety factor, but nothing says that he has to reply to us either. He isn't responding to us. Allen, on the other hand, talks quite a bit but Allen, I'm afraid, can't help us out at all. The man appears to have broken."

"Broken?"

"I never wanted him," the Director says. "It was forced down my throat by the lower echelons. I never liked that man from the start."

"I'm afraid he's not very good," Oakes agrees. "He might have gone on for years and years and none the worse for wear but there's poor tolerance to a strong stress situation here and I think the man has crossed over. It's unfortunate, a great personal tragedy, but we can't be concerned about that now. There are somewhat higher stakes here."

"I fought against him," says the Director. "No one wants to listen to you though. More or less you become a figurehead. The whole thing has been running loose for years now. People are beginning to recognize that; that's why the heat is on."

"Busby is an even more interesting figure," Oakes says. "As you can guess, we've really been into these files in recent hours. A very interesting man." He gives the Director a sidelong glance. "Is this another one you fought against?" he asks. "I imagine so."

"Well, I kept an eye—"

"In his case it could have been anticipated. All the indications are there. It had to be suicidal of you to permit a man like this into space."

"What do I know about it?" the Director mumbles. "I told you, I simply have nothing to do with the training and selection of crews."

"You would have to be mad to let Busby out there," Oakes says. "There's a lot of particular craziness there. We're going to have another look at this situation starting immediately."

"They go ahead on their own," the Director says. "Nominal authority is nothing here, you understand that, you've been around Washington long enough to understand that the chief of a department has almost nothing to do with it, that the department has an independent existence—" He breaks off, reaches for a cigarette, puts it into his mouth and scratches his head, utterly at a loss. Oakes passes him some matches; the Director lights the cigarette abstractedly at the wrong end, becomes aware of the noxious odor and grinds the butt out under his foot. "I tried," he said, "I never had a chance. They won't let you function here even if they told you enough so that you could. That's the post he gave me."

"I'm sympathetic, John," Oakes says. "I'm really moved, let me tell you."

"It's not my fault! I can tell you who's really running this place; let me turn the names over to you and make for some real accountability."

"Don't you think that the situation is too serious for accountability at this time?" Martin says. "Hasn't it gotten a little too late for self-protection?" He gets an approving nod from Oakes for this one although Oakes may only be reacting to other currents and breezes in the room. The situation, at least for Martin, has edged totally from reality; he is not sure that Oakes is anymore sane than the Director. "Tell me," Martin says, "how effective are those nuclear devices anyway?"

"That would be your department," Oakes says. "Don't you have all the facts on hand?"

"I never had any experience with them. The press releases, I never read them, I just handed them out. That was my job."

"That sounds reasonable," Oakes says. "Everybody was just doing his job, right up to the end. Even Busby. Busby is only doing his job."

"So how powerful are they?"

"Considerable," Oakes says vaguely and leans back in the chair, shaking his head. "Their power is considerable. There's a good deal of armament on that ship, more even than we conceded. There was a double payload in case of malfunctioning of one pile."

"Well," Martin says, "you see, there's nothing that I can really do." He looks at the two of them, then stares down toward the floor. "I don't even know why I'm here. There's absolutely nothing that I can do, don't you know that? I didn't put those things on the ships; that wasn't our department at all. Talk to the Pentagon. Have the Pentagon get on the wire to him and ask him to be reasonable. Use the same technique," he says, "that you used on me. That ought to be awfully effective for a man carrying around a full load of nukes."

"I told you," the Director says over him to Oakes, "I told you what we had here. He even agrees. Send the man away. This is not the answer. You'll have to work on a way to blow up the ship, that's all. They're working on it; maybe they'll come up with something. It's the only answer."

"Oh, they're working on it," Oakes says mildly. "Been working on it for hours to try to defeat their own engineering but it turns out that the engineering was pretty competent. The engineering was fine. There was a little problem with the *men* but who cares about that?" He turns back toward Martin, looks at him for a while with at least a simulation of concern and then goes to the handkerchief again. "I know your whole story," he says. "We've been into the background. Of course I was filled in from the beginning on this but I had the opportunity to do some real digging. Of course you have my sympathy, you've had a tough time."

"Sure," says Martin. "That's wonderful. Thanks very much for your understanding. It's great to hear that, let me tell you."

"Don't be bitter," Oakes says. "Amends can still be made; it isn't too late. What I mean is that it's pretty much the same thing, you and Busby. That's what we've decided. In many ways, the situations seem to pattern against one another precisely. Naturally this a more serious situation."

"Naturally."

"But there's an amazing concordance in many ways."

"I'm glad to hear it."

"We should have perhaps looked into this thing a lot more carefully. After your events there was some pressure to do so but I'm afraid that I wasn't terribly alert. We left it to our friend here but he was too busy blaming the lower echelons, which has been his pattern for a long time, long before you came along. Sometimes the whole chain of command theory doesn't work too well, I'm sorry to say. Sometimes things should be considered, questions should be asked but aren't. You tend to rest on a series of assumptions at the beginning and they underlie everything, you may not realize until too late in the game that there was something wrong with those assumptions. That they might have been wrong. Then you start to go around blaming people, which isn't very instructive either. There have been mistakes here and to a certain extent there have been only victims, nothing else. You've been one of them and for that we're sorry. But maybe it isn't too late to go back to the beginning."

"Well you see," Martin points out with enormous reasonableness, "you see, Mr. Oakes, the thing is that you were stupid. All of you. You used the word suicidal before, not me, and it's a good word. You should have called a halt to this after the last mission and had a long look at it then."

"You're too simple, Martin, if you look at it as a question of the last mission, your own problems. We should have backed off on this much further ago than that. I said that already and I meant it."

"But you didn't do any of that, did you? You wanted to pin it all on me. I was scapegoated."

"You have a right to be bitter."

"It has nothing to do with bitterness. You could have backed off on this a long time ago and saved my ass. Now it's someone else's and probably yours. I've been doing a lot of thinking about this. I'm not stupid no matter what the Director says. My education wasn't too good and I had little opportunity but I can think."

"I know you can," Oakes says gently, holding him in a stare. "You've impressed me very favorably. You're doing very well; maybe we should have listened to you instead of ourselves."

"It's too late."

"Never too late," Oakes says. "I don't believe that; we can still stop this."

"Stop bullshitting him, Oakes," the Director says. "I can't listen to much more of this."

"Keep quiet, John," Oakes says, waving a hand. "Stay out of this. This is between us now all the way through to the end. Of course Busby's a very disturbed man. We couldn't have reckoned it went this far so soon. There might be some excuse."

"And Allen?"

"Allen was a mistake," Oakes says quietly. "Both of them were mistakes. I don't know what more I can tell you. I'm not arguing."

"So you've got two mistakes and a dead man up in that capsule now. Just a little agency error. Just a few failed assumptions. You kill people and then you say the assumptions are wrong, you'll look at it a different way. That's the government, isn't it?"

"Sometimes. Sometimes. There have been errors. But the government can change. People change and with them governments as well. You can't be completely hopeless about this."

"That all depends on who you are. What do you want me to do?"

"Don't you know?"

"It's too late, Oakes. I'm on the way out. They took my commission from me and now this miserable job and I'm due out of here in three days."

"You can't think in context of days and weeks anymore, Colonel. We have a problem. We felt that you could be of some help to us. It's your problem too. In fact, it's everyone's."

"I'm supposed to think of the nukes, huh? Well, I'm too tied up with myself now to give the nukes much thought. I just can't get excited, somehow. What am I supposed to do? Get on the intercom and tell Busby that he's too nice a guy to fire the missiles?"

"Uh huh," Oakes says, nodding. "That's just about what we did have in mind. After all, if you can't talk to the man, who can? There are so many similarities. We want to work along these lines. He might be, uh, less resistant to you than to anyone else. We can give that a try."

"You won't believe this, Oakes," Martin says, "but to be quite honest, I'm just not very interested right now. Call it disassociation if you want but what Busby does is a matter of total indifference to me. I feel outside of it, see? It's not me up there; it's him and it's got to be worked out that way."

"That may be reasonable—"

"I don't know how reasonable I am anymore. I was a reasonable man for thirty-seven years and you see where that got me. Maybe it's time for a little unreason, and I just can't get excited about the agency's problem. I think of it as the agency's problem. Now this may say very little for me but that's just about the way that I'm looking this over."

"Public-spirited," the Director says. "Dependable, cooperative, helpful. That's Martin. Of course we can put him under orders."

"Threats aren't necessary," Martin says, looking directly at Oakes. "You don't have to take that tack. I didn't say that I won't give it a try."

"Good."

"If you want me to, of course I'll give it a try. I have some feeling for this man although in no way that you could understand. But I just don't care very much anymore, not about almost anything, and I don't know if you want to put that kind of a man out on the line for you. I'm being perfectly honest. My heart wouldn't be in it. I can't get enraged or excited."

"Why not?" says Oakes. "What better offer can you make? I can't talk for your psyche, your unconscious is your own business." He shoves the handkerchief deep into his pocket, stands wincing and leans over the desk. "That's fine, Colonel."

"I won't have it as part of a show," Martin says.

"Huh?"

"No monitor. No hookup. This has got to be between Busby and myself."

"Of course," Oakes says. "If you want it that way we can line the transmission between just the two of you. I'm perfectly willing to cooperate. That sounds reasonable to me."

"And no matter what happens, I don't want it to become part of the story. No hard news, no backgrounds, no in-depths. I'm finished."

"You'd be a heroic figure, Colonel."

"Fuck that," Martin says. "Fuck it. I don't think anyone cares at all. I don't think they know or are concerned and I want it to stay that way. This is part of the records of the agency. Nothing else, I mean that."

"All right," Oakes says, "if that's what you want. We might be able to arrange a bonus for you though or some assignment. You'll be compensated."

"I don't want to be compensated."

"Tough one," Oakes says. "Oh my, a tough one. They turn out real men in the program, don't they?"

They look at one another for an instant and then they begin to laugh. They laugh quite hysterically for a minute, but without bad temper or backslapping until the Director comes to attention behind the desk, begins to slam his palms on the desk, looks at them with fury and screams that the conference is at an end.

Oakes and Martin nod, wink at one another and rise to their feet still laughing. They put their arms around one another and go through the door that way, leaving the lieutenant outside, Martin hopes, in a state of thorough astonishment.

It may be mad, Martin finds himself thinking later, it may have been an act of *total* madness, but he knows now that all things considered, the laughter may have been the first truly balanced thing he has done in four or five months. The first truly balanced thing he has done in his life. The first truly balanced thing which anyone may have done forever.

XXII

All along they specified that they had to watch the obscenities.

Well, what if it had been the other way? What if they had given instead a Lecture of Authorization in the latter stages of training during which the word had been given that they could say FUCK YOU on the telecasts, SON OF A BITCH on the telecasts, BASTARD on the telecasts. What if they had let it be known that it would somehow be more dignified to approach the problem in this way?

Maybe, if they had allowed them all of this, no one would have come to grief. Maybe it could have worked out the cheap, easy way and the things inside him or the others would never have come to the surface. They had only been able to keep outside of themselves. Letting them speak freely would have helped this along.

Asepsis was not the answer, not when a good obscenity could take you so far. When you came right down to it, it would not even have been necessary to have broadcast the obscenities; they could have put a block on the transmissions. If freedom had been granted, he might never have had to use it. If only the opportunity had been theirs it might have worked out all right.

He has never understood why the center would not let them curse. Granted, it was on a media hook-up and this is a government project, one of the biggest. Still the government was not putting into this a twentieth of what is put into the war every year; they could have let them go a little way on their own. Space was, when you thought about it, an entirely new experience: they should have allowed them to work into it in entirely different ways. None of the old rules could apply in the new circuit; space was no freeway, spacemen were not pilots. But they would not go along with that, they had insisted that space be a continuation of the same rules and they had done their job well up to a point. On the way out, when he had still had his senses, Martin had looked out of the craft's portholes, half-expecting to see the flat, dense gray of the highway before him and on one side, in the far distance, the beckoning wink of a motel or an all-purpose food stand welcoming him to dine in comfort. The Moon, they wanted the Moon to be a motel.

Something had become part of the folklore of the space program which all of them had heard. In the earlier days it was said that a man had been yanked off the crew right before the countdown because someone had tipped them off to the man's plans to say something graphic in space. "I'm going to say," this man had threatened his source, "what I'm going to say when we pull into Moon orbit, I'm going to say, baby, I'd like to be going down on you right this minute. I'm a quarter of a million miles out, swimming in space, and I'm still dreaming of your tits. You've got a pair of tits that a man would like to take to the Moon, that's what I'm going to say to the bitch," the man had bragged and his source (who might have been one of the crewmates or maybe an overseer planting devices in his quarters for central staff) had turned him right in, turned him in to the top and the man had been taken off this flight on twelve hours notice with the covering word that he had been exposed to a contagious illness and that unnecessary risks could not be taken at this stage of the mission, no matter how small the risks might be.

The man literally never got over it. He could not understand it, he could understand nothing, he had wandered through the program in somnolence for three or four months after that—

telling everyone that he could have been the nineteenth man on the Moon, that that part of him was already on the Moon irrevocably lost, he would never recover himself again—and then had been quietly pensioned to some plant where he had become a quality-control supervisor of minor technicians, still used for the giving of occasional interviews to the local press when new missions were launched in the years ahead.

"But she was my *wife*," he had told the Director when called up for the hearing, "the girl was my wife, what's wrong with wishing your wife well and, anyway, I never would have done it. I was only kidding. Did they think that I was really crazy enough to do something like that and risk this program?"

The man's face had contracted to astonishment. He seemed to be trapped in one reflexive mood forever and whether or not this folklore was true—there was a contradictory tale that he had come up with a sudden, severe, disastrous drop on one of the psychological-performance tests and they had not wanted to take any risks while needing at the same time to save his ego—they had been very careful of their speculations not to say their language in space from that time in. No astronaut ever cursed or if he did he would deny it.

There had to be another way to do it. That was the way Martin saw the thing, that was the feeling of maybe a few of the others but as to what that way would be and where it would have gotten them . . . he did not know. Nor could he discuss it with the others; that was something you did not share.

There was something to be said for the preservation of space as a moral quality inimical to the old obscenities and laxity but on the other hand, it had to seem like a hell of a waste of opportunity. The fact was that you never knew. You could never make a positive and final calculation, there was never a point at which one way or the other you knew what had to be done and the time of alternative was over. No one had had that happen in the history of the project right up until Busby who, it seemed, had made his choice, God bless him.

The rest of them: the rest of them might never know what was going on inside if they stayed lucky. Luck was the name of the game; if it held out you could avoid the knowing for a long time. Possibly for all time and that was for the best. Then you never had to come to terms with the problem of space. Space was just an extension of the training procedures which were an extension of everything the government had ever told you about what kind of person you were and what role you occupied in the scheme of things.

Walking over to the communications center, almost hand-in-hand with Oakes, Martin realizes that he never thought about space at all, not until the very end on the fifth time around and then it came with such a rush of complication that space seemed to be something else. Call it love. Call it loss. But never give it its real name. Because it had none that we could give it.

XXIII

In a pocket, he sits alone as if in a dream.

The whir of equipment is around him: technicians in the background, the whine of machinery. Oakes is out there too, maybe supervising, but Oakes is already gone. He knows he will never see him again. Martin is alone.

They have assured him that his voice will be heard in the capsule; whether or not Busby will answer is another issue. There is even a hint of opinion that Busby may be somehow dead but Martin knows this is nonsense. In similar circumstances he was alive, now he would be making plans. One did not go so far so irrevocably for death. He tests the microphone, which is soundless, and talks into the equipment, seeing by the movement of small lights that his voice is making patterns; the patterns cascade like ribbons over the surface of the machinery, moving in many shapes and colors.

"Listen, Busby," he says, "listen to me. This is Martin. Remember? You hear me, don't you? I know you hear me. You want to hear me.

"Busby," he says, "do you want my wife? You could have had her, you know. Maybe you could yet. She's all yours, Busby, she left me already. Maybe she wants you. I don't object. You can have her if you want. Think about this.

"Do you hear me, Busby?" he says, leaning toward the console, feeling the intensity overtake him. "It's really true. It's all right. You can have her, do you hear me? The whole thing is over now."

There is a thump. Busby's voice, flat, mechanical, comes on. He says, "I hear you, Martin."

"Good."

"I said I heard you. That's all. It's too late for any of that."

"Only if you think so."

"I don't know who your wife is, Martin," Busby says. "I don't know what you're talking about. I'm a busy man, I got lots of problems, got a dead man on this capsule beginning to stink and another who cries all the time. Can't listen to romantic babble now. Work out your own solutions. In the little time you have left. Don't talk anymore."

"Busby," Martin says, "Busby, listen to me. Just listen."

"I've got to think. Don't you hear me, I want to *think*!"

"Don't fail me, Busby," Martin says, leaning close to the equipment. "Don't fail me now. Don't start to think, you got so far just by not thinking, don't foul it up now. Drop the fucking things, Busby. Head back and drop those fuckers."

"Oh God."

"God, God, you *must*, don't you see? You can't go this far just to stop. Hold on for another twelve hours, kill Allen if you have to, jettison Davis, don't lose it all now. Drop the fuckers," Martin says. "Drop it. Do it!"

"Don't know. Don't know."

"Got to do it, Busby, wanted to do it myself but couldn't quite make it, turned out that I was one of their goddamned machines, they had their hooks in too deep. But I came close. You can go all the way. Don't listen. Don't listen to any more. Just do it."

"I'll try," Busby whispers. "I tell you I'll try, it's just that the voices—"

"Hold on," Martin says, "hold on, hold to yourself, just do it," and then he begins to sing, has no clear idea of why he chose to sing at this moment but the words make sense. "You're tired and cold but you can stay bold," he sings to Busby and then begins the obscenities, he tells Busby every dirty word in the English language that he can bring to mind, quickly, and in fast combinations, he begins to sing about vessels and tassels and rockets and pockets and there is no way, no way that Busby can override him because this is the irrevocable audio and he feels hands at him, arms prying, he is dragged back from the console with terrific force, still fighting to get the last words in and then they are all looking at him, technicians, scientists, Oakes, a general in full dress, backing away from the touch now as if he were bleeding and there is a small abscess of clarity in which he can drop what he wants to say; he says, "It won't work, don't you see? It won't work. It's just too late and all meant to be this way because this is the way you wanted it. This is what you built and you're just going to have to take the full consequences so leave me out of it, you motherfuckers," and falls through their arms toward the floor (he is really quite tired) and finds himself thinking how strange it is, how really peculiar, that Busby has held out this long only for the possibility of remorse. His wife may have had something to do with that; it is her own pattern. How strange, how strange, Richard Martin dreams and then he—

—hits the floor and for a long, long time does no thinking at all although with the omnipresent administrations of the dedicated and competent medical staff he is brought back to full, raving consciousness in plenty of time for the final act which is at this moment (although he does not know it) exactly thirty-six hours and twenty-five minutes away . . . and counting.

AFTERWORD
THE FALLING ASTRONAUTS IN CONTEXT: MAD SPACEMEN AND NUCLEAR BOMBS

Umberto Rossi

> Little information has been released about the psychological effects of space travel. . . . But it is clear from the subsequently troubled careers of many of the astronauts . . . that they suffered severe psychological damage.
>
> —J.G. Ballard, Commentary on *The Atrocity Exhibition*

> Ashes to ashes, funk to funky
> We know Major Tom's a junkie
> Strung out in heaven's high
> Hitting an all-time low
>
> —David Bowie, "Ashes to Ashes"

In order to fully appreciate the novel you have just finished reading, we must go back in time and situate it in its historical context. It is difficult to appreciate how iconoclastic and subversive *The Falling Astronauts* was when it was published without considering the hopes and expectations surrounding the US space program in the sf community—tremendously difficult in a time like ours, when so many people either believe that we have never been on the Moon or do not care at all. Besides, let us not forget that Barry N. Malzberg is both a maverick, dissident sf writer *and* a sf columnist and editor with a wide knowledge of the genre. Any attempt to understand his oeuvre cannot disregard the milieu of previous and contemporary sf.

Moreover, Malzberg is the paradigmatic New Wave writer—not as celebrated and lucky as J. G. Ballard, who managed to escape the sf ghetto in the 1980s, and not as circumfused with myth as Philip K. Dick—but as representative of that movement as it comes, so much so that Roger Luckhurst had to mention him (with Ballard) as an emblematic representative of New Wave's dislike of outer space and the Space Race. But when we talk about the New Wave, we deal with a movement that rebelled against the tradition of sf as it had been defined during the Golden Age, so that his works must be always read as deconstructing or demolishing one or several myths of that tradition. And I tend to agree with Thomas M. Disch when he posits the starship as the central myth of sf; hence the archetypal sf hero is the spaceman, the space traveler, the astronaut (with the alien as his or her negative image).

A sound understanding of a genuinely New Wave novel like *The Falling Astronauts* necessitates the recollection of a series of astronauts who go where no man has gone before, but also go insane. Mad astronauts appeared in sf long before those portrayed by Malzberg. However, the treatment of madness in connection with space flight by previous authors was quite different.

In 1959, CBS broadcast the pilot episode of the inaugural season of *The Twilight Zone*, one of its most famous and scariest. Written by Rod Serling, "Where Is Everybody?" features Mike Ferris, an astronaut who has entered an extended and fearful hallucination in which he is the only person in an empty world. This delusional state has not been caused by real space flight, but by a sadistic form of training, as Ferris has been kept in isolation for 484 hours on Earth. The story implies that the plight of the astronaut is so extreme that madness is a sort of occupational disease that can affect spacemen even *before* they are launched. The fact that this initial episode dealt with astronauts and space flight should not come as a surprise: "Where Is Everybody?" was aired on October 2, 1959, almost two years after Sputnik 1 had been launched on October 4, 1957, when space was all the rage.

The episode ends on an optimistic note despite Ferris' nightmarish delusion. Recovering his sanity, the astronaut tells the moon: "Hey! Don't go away up there! Next time it won't be a dream or a nightmare. Next time it'll be for real. So don't go away. We'll be up there in a little while." The moral is that astronauts may experience moments of insanity, but ultimately reason, courage, and goodness will prevail.

A bleaker but nonetheless dignified version of such a moral had been expressed before the pilot of *The Twilight Zone* was aired in James E. Gunn's "Space is a Lonely Place" (1957), a novelette where the madness of astronauts may be permanent and irreparable. On the *Santa Maria* (mind the name!), the first spaceship flying to Mars, crew members go insane, one by one, eventually killing each other or committing suicide before reaching the Red Planet. Gunn effectively depicts the gradual deterioration of the astronauts' minds, although many of the scientific and technological details sound outdated today. Still, the crew of the *Santa Maria*, deranged as they may be, exhibits valor and grit. Holloway, Craddock, Burr, Jelinek and Migliardo are heroes overwhelmed by an exceedingly long confinement and the strain of the space mission. They are martyrs who die for a good cause.

Once the spaceship reaches Mars, it "will be sending back telemetered reports from its telescopic examination of the surface, from its sounding missiles"; it will also "conduct geological explorations, analyze samples and telemeter back their finding," as one of the Mars mission managers comfortingly explains. Gunn goes so far as to suggest that the ship itself is the perfect astronaut, with no "neuroses, no tummy aches, no weakness, no indecision, no space-madness." Of course, as another character objects, "Man's representatives . . . must be living, breathing, fearful men like themselves." Some day the red planet must be reached by men, not only machines. In the meantime, notwithstanding the death of the astronauts, the mission is a technological success because the *Santa Maria* worked perfectly. The sacrifice of the five spacemen is not in vain; they may have gone mad, but theirs is a heroic madness: "Men died for the Western Hemisphere, to tame the Antarctic, to develop atomic power, to build skyscrapers and roads. Men died to build the Little Wheel and the Big Wheel. Space is hungry, too. And men stick their heads in its mouth because they're men."

The conclusion of the story indicates that there will be spacemen capable of reaching the other planets of the Solar System, then coming back. It will be the sons of commander Lloyd, who were born and raised in the space station, and who consider space and confinement in an orbital station (or a spaceship) their natural environment.

There are other examples of astronauts who plunge into madness due to the overwhelming psychological stress of space travel. Suffice it to mention a British novel that reads like a collection of linked stories, John Wyndham's *The Outward Urge* (1959), whose third and fifth chapter ("Mars: A.D. 2094" and "The Emptiness of Space, The Asteroids: A.D. 2194") both feature mad astronauts. They may go insane and may even act insanely, but they should be perceived as casualties in an extremely dangerous yet necessary enterprise. If mankind wants to conquer space, a price must be paid; people will go insane, die, be crippled. But their sacrifice will pave the way to the stars.

Another remarkable specimen of this idea is Theodore Sturgeon's 1959 short story "The Man Who Lost the Sea," portraying a failed mission to Mars through the modernist technique of destructured stream-of-consciousness and flashback that is associated with a rare second-person narrative. This sophisticated tale culminates in the moment when the dying protagonist realizes that "the satellite fading here is Phobos, that those footprints are your own, that there is no sea here, that you have crashed and are killed and will in a moment be dead." The gloomy ending is redeemed by the feelings of joy that overwhelm the fading consciousness of the dying astronaut when "he takes his triumph at the other side of death" because the enterprise managed to carry man to another planet. Hence the final cry of the protagonist: "God, we made it!"

Since the times of *Beowulf*, the sacrifice of the hero has always been part of epic narratives. These stories belong to an epic of space conquest that is quite common in the sf of the 1950s, which foregrounds the human cost of the conquest of space. We do not have the escapist fantasies of the 1920s and 1930s any more. This may have to do with the fact that, at the end of the 50s, space seemed much closer than before. The context of the Cold War involves the recurrence of astronauts' heroic sacrifice. In fact, nuclear war features in Gunn's *Station in Space* (the 1958 collection that included "Space is a Lonely Place") as well as Wyndham's *The Outward Urge* (1959). The war is actually more of a hindrance for both writers, as the destination of humankind is outer space and astronauts cannot be bothered with megadeath and fallout, yet it is part of the picture of the future histories presented to readers. Furthermore, the ethics of sacrifice seem to be connected with the logic of sacrifice detected by Adam Piette in several Cold War narratives; it is particularly evident in a novel on the borderline between sf and mainstream like Eugene Burdick and Harvey Wheeler's *Fail-Safe* (1962).

When the US space program officially started, images of the dangers of space travel (entailing death, suffering and madness) were definitely not what NASA wanted to project and circulate in the mediascape. In her dense monograph *Rocket States*, Fabienne Collignon persuasively argues that Cape Canaveral embodies "a terminal, bleached dreamworld of absolute security, tranquility." Security appears to be the main concern of the American space program, which Collignon reads in the wider context of the Cold War. Her analysis of technology and, above all, technological imagination and discourses, shows how the rhetoric of NASA pivots on rationality and predictability, on the implementation of safe and predictable systems. There is no space in such discourses (and the actual space missions NASA carried out) for the heroic figure of the astronaut as depicted in Wyndham, Gunn and Sturgeon's stories. And there is no space at all for the mad astronaut (not even the one who recovers sanity imagined by Rod Serling).

Ideally the astronaut should have been a cyborg, a hybrid being conceived of not by a sf writer but by two scientists, both researchers at the Rockland State Hospital, Manfred E. Clynes and Nathan S. Kline. In their 1960 essay "Cyborgs and Space," Clynes and Kline say that reproducing the natural environment in space is too expensive and too complicated. Instead human beings should be modified to live in space. "If man attempts partial adaptation to space conditions, instead of insisting on carrying his whole environment along with him, a number of new possibilities appear." Mankind must be (re)made like the components of those weapon systems that were being developed in those years, the space program and the arms race being, after all, two sides of the same coin.

Let us not forget that the same man who was managing the construction of the Saturn V rocket that brought astronauts to the Moon, Wernher Von Braun, is the father of the PGM-11 Redstone, the first large American ballistic missile (launched in 1953). The Redstone was also used to launch Alan Shepard and Gus Grissom in their 1961 sub-orbital flights. Like the Saturn rocket, Intercontinental Ballistic Missiles were complex, sophisticated weapon systems "designed to insure that all major factors in the . . . effort were traced in terms of their complex interrelationships and not in isolation," as Robert L. Perry explained in an article on rocket technology published in 1963. If these documents express the prevailing mentality in the US space program, clearly there is no place in space for heroes: astronauts are just cogs in a machine, "factors" whose behavior must be predictable and dependable.

Collignon stresses the passivity of astronauts—not aviators or aces (or enterprising captains or spacemen on spaceships), but "passive subjects" in a pod. Or, to put it in Tom Wolfe's words, "laboratory animals wired up from skull to rectum with medical sensors." While more "adult" and mature than the Space Opera of the 1930s and 1940s, the cosmic adventure of Gunn's, Wyndham's and Sturgeon's stories has turned into a carefully programmed routine, a clockwork mission where everything takes place at the right moment on a predictable schedule. Only Apollo 13 injected some elements of suspense into a program that was a little boring. No wonder that the unlucky Apollo mission of Lowell, Swigert and Heise seems to be the only one that managed to survive in the collective memory after the first, triumphal flight and moon landing of Apollo 11.

This aside by Ballard comes to mind: "Even before the Space Age had begun I had a hunch it would be short-lived—basically because NASA and the Russians had left the imagination out of space, one mistake the sf writers never made." Not that such a sceptical approach to the space race of the 1960s and early 1970s was typical of all sf readers, writers and critics; Armstrong, Collins and Aldrin's 1970 celebratory book *First on the Moon* had an epilogue written by Arthur C. Clarke.

Many practitioners of the genre shared the stance expressed by sf scholar Gary Westfahl:

Like many science-fiction readers of my generation, first captivated in my youth by Robert A. Heinlein's juveniles, I long considered myself an advocate of human space exploration. I attentively followed the American space program in the 1960s, cheered when Spiro Agnew proposed a manned Mars expedition during the Apollo 11 flight, and lamented the stagnation and hesitancy of American space activities after the Apollo program.

Additionally, Westfahl wrote a critical study, *Islands in the Sky: The Space Station Theme in Science Fiction Literature,* that was overtly in favour of an extensive space program.

Yet there were malcontents in the sf community. One of them was J.G. Ballard with his powerful, visionary short stories on dead astronauts, including "The Cage of Sand" (1962), "Memories of the Space Age" (1982) and, above all, "The Dead Astronaut" (1968), which may well have been a source of inspiration for Malzberg when he wrote *The Falling Astronauts.*

Ballard's provocative ideas inspired other sf writers, among them Robert Silverberg. His novella *The Feast of St. Dionysus* (1972) portrays an astronaut who is quite far from the spotless, fearless heroes of Apollo 11 and a mission that was definitely not a glorious success. The protagonist, Oxenshuer, is the only survivor of a catastrophic mission to Mars; the rest of the three-man crew perished in a sandstorm. He feels guilty about the death of his companions, Richardson and Vogel, whose bodies he left on Mars, and he is tormented by his love for Claire, the widow of Vogel, his friend and crewmate. The fact that Mars was reached and at least one of the astronauts managed to get back does not redeem the failure. Palsied with remorse, Oxenshuer ventures into the Mojave desert on foot, looking for atonement: "That gray, pervasive sense of guilt, heavy on him since his return from Mars, held less weight here beyond civilization's edge. This wasteland was the closest he could come to attaining Mars on Earth. Not really close enough ... But it was as close ... as he could manage."

Oxenshuer quests for a sort of inner Mars, an alien world that only exists in the vortex of his tortured mind. What he finds is a strange community of Dionysians living in a desert village that is also a labyrinth distinguished by mysterious rituals involving wrestling and wine. The villagers worship Dionysus, who is also Christ, and when Oxenshuer joins their community, they tell him that he "will enter the ocean of Christ" in the middle of the Mojave Desert. When the moment of his initiation comes, he falls into a hallucinatory state that brings him back to Mars shortly after the disaster that killed his crewmates. Oxenshuer retrieves the corpses of the two dead astronauts so that they can be returned to Earth.

Is this mere wish-fulfilment or a sort of psychedelic trip triggered not by wine but by LSD? Is this a travel into inner space that somehow heals the trauma suffered in outer space? In the end, when Oxenshuer tries to go back to the Dionysian village, not alone this time but with Claire, he cannot find it. The suggestion is that it might have all been a delusion. Regardless, the delusion managed to heal the mental wounds of the astronauts. More interesting is the fact that, while the US space program was somewhat protected by Apollo, the solar god of reason (as suggested by David A. Lanyon in his reading of Malzberg's sf), Oxenshuer must resort to the worshipper of a god that, according to Nietzsche, was his complementary opposite: Dionysus, the god of drunkenness, ritual madness and religious ecstasy. If, as we shall see, Malzberg takes us beyond Apollo, in his demolition of the rationality of the space program, Silverberg places himself and his deranged astronaut *against* Apollo, on the side of Dionysian madness.

Silverberg makes it clear that the pinpoint precision of the mission schedule killed the two astronauts; in fact, when Vogel proposes to change the program and go out for the "ninety-kilo-meter-crawler-jaunt" to the Gulliver site at the beginning of their stay on Mars (not on Day Twenty, as decreed by the mission timetable), he is trying to overrule the inflexible order imposed by Mission Control. The astronaut would like to regain at least a modicum of autonomy, to stop being an individual subsystem integrated in the great clockwork machine of the Mars mission, but Oxenshuer hesitates "to deviate from the schedule." Thus he and Richardson accept the passive role (of laboratory animals) devised for them by NASA so that the EVA takes place on Day Twenty and the two astronauts head bumpily towards their death. No wonder that, after such a failure of rationality in the mission schedule and the ban on any form of improvisation, Ox-enshuer feels he has to forsake Apollo and join a Dionysian cult. The mad astronaut is both a product of an over-rationalized space program, a victim of an alienating and instrumental rationality, and a reaction to it, an escape from the custodial machinations of the Apollo program.

It is not the only contradiction we find in the sf of the 1970s. In *The Seven Beauties of Science Fiction*, Istvan Csicsery-Ronay Jr. maintains that "the astronauts are the quintessential Handy Man," one of the most recent embodiments of a figure with an archetypal value, someone "usually male, who possesses skill in the handling of tools." The genealogy of such a character stretches back to Odysseus, who is usually defined in Homer's poem as *polymechanos* (πολυμήχανος), meaning full of re-sources, inventive, ever-ready. Csicsery-Ronay Jr. refers to the heroic astronauts à la Gunn, Wyndham and Sturgeon as well as their forerunners in Golden Age sf, which were much greater than life, such as John W. Campbell's Aarn Munro.

There is an implicit contradiction in Csicsery-Ronay Jr.'s anal-ysis. He notices that the astronauts "are even viewed as disorient-ingly automatic" and "are shown lacking poetic imagination . . .

but they are the perfect, austere, self-sacrificing subjects of Enlightenment." Additionally, as Handy Men, they should "demonstrate their handiness," their skills in the handling of extremely advanced tools. But the space capsules and the Saturn rockets are controlled by someone else: Mission Control. Most of the time, the astronauts are passive. Only when something goes wrong (as on Apollo 13) can they "demonstrate their handiness in very Crusoe-like ways, constructing life-saving devices out of the scraps left in the shipwreck."

The problem, then, is that a tradition of sf that depicts astronauts as dynamic, heroic actors involved in a dangerous enterprise clashes with the reality of the US space program, which was distinguished by predictability, subordination, and passivity (the thesis of Tom Wolfe's *The Right Stuff*, incidentally). Malzberg exploited this contradiction with remarkable results in *The Falling Astronauts*, published just two years after the first Moon landing and a year after the troubled Apollo 13 mission. Although the acronym NASA and the word "Apollo" never appear in the text, the anonymous agency and the nameless program mirror the historical ones: space capsules with three-man crews reach the moon, two astronauts land on the surface, and the third member of the crew waits for them in orbit. What has already happened when the novel begins, however, and what is slowly revealed through a series of flashbacks, does not belong to history as we know it: the nervous breakdown suffered by the protagonist, Colonel Richard Martin, as he orbits the Moon. This moment of insanity is the climax of a growing unease. Repeatedly Martin asks himself what would happen, what would they do to him, if he pressed the retrofire button, abandoned the mission and returned to Earth, leaving his two crewmates behind to die. When the unease turns into a stark mental disorder, Martin hears the retrofire button talking to him "in a small but manic voice," tempting him to do the deed, to "take a chance," and justifying the insane act. "THEY'LL CALL IT TECHNICAL MALFUNC-TION ANYWAY AND YOU'LL BE CALLED TWICE A HERO FOR MANAGING TO ESCAPE WITH YOUR LIFE," says the voice. "DO IT, COME ON, NOTHING TO LOSE."

Martin begins to rave and Mission Control attempts to stabilize him, but it isn't so easy. All they can do is talk to him. Assisted by the Director himself, Mission Control ultimately succeeds, but Martin's career as an astronaut is over. To hush up the accident, NASA, rather than fire him, reassigns him to the purely symbolic position of information officer. The anomaly (i.e., the mad astronaut) is thus normalized and neutralized. The reporters Martin has to meet are "docile, cooperative, amenable"—under control. Moon landings are routine and no longer newsworthy. As Martin informs the journalists, "Everything is on schedule . . . Everything is go-normal . . . Everything is great." Order reigns (once more) in Cape Canaveral.

Martin's bout with madness is an act of rebellion. Remember that the retrofire button tells him to "SHOW THEM THAT YOU ARE A MAN AND NOT A ROBOT. SHOW THEM THAT THEY CAN'T PUSH A MAN LIKE YOU AROUND WITH THEIR GODDAMNED SILLY ORDERS AND ARROGANCE BUT THAT YOU'VE GOT A MIND OF YOUR OWN AND YOU CANNOT BE TRIFLED WITH." We can apply to *The Falling Astronauts* something Layton said about a later novel by Malzberg, *Beyond Apollo*: "[T]he type of the . . . machine mind astronauts are supposed to have is somehow sick and insane." But madness in this novel is not caused by the stress of space flight or by traumatic experiences in space or on other planets, as it is in the stories of Gunn, Wyndham and even Silverberg. *It is the space program itself that has driven Martin insane.* This is said quite clearly when, during the humiliating meeting with the Director in chapter 13, the former astronaut vents his feelings:

Do you know what it's like to be locked up in a training mission? . . . Do you know what it's like to spend six weeks living in a cubicle with two other men, two adult males? . . . Do you know what it's like in a simular? . . . When you get ten gravities on you, the eyeballs feel like you're imploding, just dropping into the sockets and draining into the mouth cavity. Ten gravities also does interesting things to your balls if you get it three times a week for a month.

However, Martin's psychotic rebellion belongs to the narrative past of the novel. We might say that the real protagonist of the story is Busby. He draws Martin's attention because he sees Busby as "a mystery." We are told that "there was some talk of Busby dropping out of the project when his wife died." His lack of visible emotions impresses Martin, who is increasingly fascinated by and almost attracted to him. "Martin should get to know Busby; of all the men in the project, Busby may be the one to whom he has the most to say at this time." The reason for this desirability emerges only when Busby overreacts to a reporter's remarks during a press conference. In space, he kills Davis, one of his crewmates, and takes control of the capsule. Paralyzed by fear, Allen, the commander, is totally unable to stop Busby.

Madness has erupted again, but this time the disruption of the schedule is much worse, as the "ship is going up with enough nuclear armaments to destroy a bloody continent," according to the reporter who enrages Busby. He's right; later in the novel, Oakes, a high-ranking government administrator, says: "There's a good deal of armament on that ship, more even than we conceded." The official explanation is that the nuclear bombs are to be used in a seismic experiment, but a military purpose is suspected (and we are also told that the Agency is under the direct control of the Department of Defense). Once

Busby has taken the capsule in hand, the overwhelming question regards what he will do with those weapons.

In a last-minute, desperate attempt to restore order, Oakes, who has superseded the Director of the Agency, asks Martin to talk to Busby. "After all, if you can't talk to the man, who can? There are so many similarities. . . . He might be, uh, less resistant to you than to anyone else." The result of this attempt confirms the similarities between Busby and Martin, reifying their identity. Busby operates as Martin's alter-ego; they are both insane, and their madness is a symptom of the alienating rules of the Agency. "Got to do it, Busby," shouts Martin, "wanted to do it myself but couldn't quite make it, turned out that I was one of their goddamned machines, they had their hooks in too deep. But I came close, you can go all the way. Don't listen. Don't listen to any more. Just do it." This is not, of course, what Oakes and the Director wanted Martin to tell Busby, but it is surely what Martin thinks. In madness is freedom.

In *The Falling Astronauts*, Malzberg cultivates an atmosphere of barely contained hysteria with grotesque, surreal scenes, including the narrator's dreams (or, better, nightmares), like the press conference in the third chapter where the "mad-eyed reporter" asks all the embarrassing questions that "real" reporters never ask. The fact that we are not offered a real ending is consistent with the overall tone of the novel: the texts stops when "the final act [whatever it may be] is . . . exactly thirty-six hours and twenty-five minutes away . . . and counting." Will Busby use the atomic weapons to wreak havoc on the Earth? Will the Agency manage to defuse this psychiatric and nuclear threat? All in all, Malzberg's novel is about the US space program as well as the Cold War. As in the previously discussed stories by Gunn and Wyndham, Malzberg sees a deep, intimate connection between the two. Connections of this nature mirror historical realities, such as Wernher von Braun's campaign for an armed space station in the early 1950s, and the much more concrete R-36ORB missile built by the USSR and deployed from 1969 to 1983, a weapon system that made nuclear bombing from space a reality. Malzberg's treatment of the alliance between the Cold War and the US space program is much less reassuring than those of the former authors; the allegorical story of Martin and Busby is not placed in the frame of a long-term future history. Unlike Wyndham, Malzberg does not console us by showing how humankind will be able to survive the nuclear holocaust.

Besides, there is another plateau of meaning in the novel where the Agency represents an anamorphic image of America, whose citizens are all astronauts, mad and alienated like Martin and Busby. In this classical metonymical displacement, a part of the country (the Agency, i.e., NASA) stands for the whole nation—something that the very metaphor of the New Frontier launched by President Kennedy made possible and also quite clear to contemporary readers. Malzberg suggests that we astronauts are all little cogs in a gigantic machine that facilitates pathology and death. Surely this is not a message that could be accepted by the sf community, which was celebrating the daring feats of the Apollo missions and saw it as a "prelude to space," to cite the title of a novel by Arthur C. Clarke.

According to sf writer Bob Shaw, Malzberg's *Beyond Apollo*, published in 1972, was "the epitome of everything that has gone wrong with sf in the last ten years or so." This rather harsh judgement could also apply to *The Falling Astronauts*. Shaw wasn't alone; a large part of sf readers, authors and editors regarded Malzberg's iconoclastic, clinically hysterical treatment of astronauts, the space program and space in general with similar indignation.

To fully appreciate Malzberg's attack on the figure of the astronaut as both the archetypal protagonist of sf "adventures" and the (anti)hero of the New Frontier, we must take into account

Beyond Apollo as well as *Revelations*, which came out the same year. Together with *The Falling Astronauts*, they form what we can effectively refer to as the Mad Astronaut Trilogy.

To some extent, *Beyond Apollo* is a sequel to *Revelations* despite an unexplained gap (something you don't find in other sf cycles) since there's no mention of what happened to Busby and his nuclear weapons. However, it seems that Armageddon did not take place, after all. There has been a mission to Mars. It was a total failure, but there is no detailed description of it. Then a Venus mission was attempted with a two-man crew in order to save money. Evans, the narrator of the novel (or rather, the author) is the only survivor. The Captain never came back.

Evans is confined to what may well be an asylum or military penitentiary. A neurologist, Claude Forrest, interrogates him. Everybody wants to know what happened to the Captain, if he and Evans reached Venus, if there is intelligent life on the planet, and so on. Evans answers Forrest's questions with ostensible candor, but he keeps changing his story. In one story, the Captain commits suicide. In another, the telepathic inhabitants of Venus compel the Captain to kill himself. In still another, Evans kills him. The different versions of what took place are, of course, mutually inconsistent. Forrest resorts to threats in hopes of squeezing out the truth . . . to no avail. Evans always conjures a new version to be discarded the next day.

Detained in an institution and "treated" by a doctor, the seemingly pathological astronaut leaves readers little choice but to treat him as an unreliable narrator. At the same time, Malzberg suggests that he may only be feigning madness because he knows something so terrible that it must not be revealed. If there is an example of postmodern ontological uncertainty in a narrative, I cannot think of a more radical one than *Beyond Apollo*. Again we have an astronaut who may or may not be insane, but in this case, Malzberg doesn't merely satirize the mentality (or dream, or nightmare) of total control and rationality indicative of the space program (notice that "Beyond Apollo" refers to both the Apollo missions and the Greek solar god of reason). In fact, Evans informs us right from the start that he plans to write a novel of the voyage and describes the Captain as he will be depicted in it. As the author, too, Evans is simultaneously an unreliable astronaut, an unreliable narrator, and an unreliable novelist. The book ends on a brazen metanarrational note with a letter from an editor of the press that intends to publish Evans' novel—whose title is, unsurprisingly, *Beyond Apollo*.

This reading can be pushed further if we perceive Evans as an avatar for Malzberg himself, spinning a series of aborted space-travel narratives. From this vantage point, Evans/Malzberg attacks the archetypal hero of classic sf with searing sarcasm while portraying himself as an apostate sf author who revels in tearing down the playhouse of the Old Guard, conjuring and then discarding the classical devices, themes and expectations of the genre.

The third novel in the Mad Astronaut Trilogy, *Revelations*, illustrates how pervasive the figure of the insane astronaut can be. A former space jockey, Walter Monaghan, contacts a TV program called "Revelations" to tell "the Full Story of the agency." Monaghan seems to be an older version of Martin in *The Falling Astronauts*. In a letter to the TV program that opens the novel, he explains: "[U]ntil my recent discharge . . . from the program . . . I . . . worked my way into one of those pointless liaison jobs which were created for ex-astronauts who got caught in the depression and had nowhere to go." Thus the first chapter gestures towards the first novel of the trilogy, but what follows is focused on the life of Hurwitz, one of the assistants of TV star Marvin Martin.

The latter is a TV talk show host who achieved celebrity thanks to *Revelations*, a (then) maverick show in which guests are aggressively, sadistically interrogated by Martin and must answer embarrassing questions about their private life. Hurwitz selects the guests, looking for people who have something out-rageous to tell—possibly something shameful—and he at first dismisses Monaghan with a brief aside: "Fuck it. I've got enough creeps already." Reading the novel, which delves into the work-ings of reality TV long before *The Real World* and *Big Brother*, we almost forget about Monaghan and his insights regarding the corruption and misery of the space program and its astro-nauts. When ratings decline, Marvin Martin urges Hurwitz to find more interesting guests. He retrieves Monaghan's letter and interviews him.

Hurwitz notices a jarring inconsistency in Monaghan's state-ments about the space program. He maintains that "we have never gone to the moon . . . [E]verything . . . was contrived by the government to appear as if we had accomplished what we hadn't through the cunning use of the media and photographic techniques." A few days later, though, he admits that "twelve of the sixty-eight men who have actually flown to the moon are now incurably insane . . . It is the very quality of the moon expe-rience which has done this to them. . . . There's no consistency! They don't jibe!" Hurwitz resembles Evans, the unreliable as-tronaut in *Beyond Apollo*, linking the three parts of the trilogy.

Monaghan shoots Marvin Martin during a live broadcast. We (and Hurwitz) discover that he is an imposter who has been implanted with false memories of his life as an astronaut. Monaghan has never been a spaceman, but he honestly believes he used to be, reminiscing Scranton, the mythomaniac in J.G. Ballard's 1985 story "The Man Who Walked on the Moon."

Much could be said about the projection of Monaghan onto the figures of other, real and purportedly deranged murderers, like Lee Harvey Oswald (there is a premonitory reference to the Dallas assassination in chapter 11). *Revelations* anticipates the conspiracy theories denying the reality of the Moon landing. The astronaut has became a sort of freak to be exploited on a TV program whose purposes "seem less informational than barbaric." Martin "has used the format only to reduce participants . . . to shattered masks who, shambling parodies of themselves, seem barely capable of human speech." The machinery of TV looks as crushing and alienating as the apparatus of the space agency in *The Falling Astronauts*. What is more relevant to us is the fact that an ordinary man, a nobody like Monaghan, can be turned into an astronaut. And it is he, the bogus spaceman, that is applied to Marvin Martin. Before pulling his gun on Martin, Monaghan accuses him of having never really listened to the answers of the guests on his show. "[Y]ou are listening to the sound of your own voice, that's all: like an astronaut, the tinny, tiny sound of your own voice reverberating back to you endlessly, the echoes collapsing in and out of your skull."

Malzberg's novels, then, serve multiple purposes, satirizing Golden Age sf and its heroic myth of the astronaut, who is dignified even when he goes insane, and attacking the US space program and its philosophy, not to mention its hidden purpose. In addition, they are salient critiques of America and Western society on the whole where the plight of the astronaut becomes a metaphor for all of our lives in an alienating, alienated civilization. We are all astronauts, it is true—mad spacemen and spacewomen like Martin and Evans or, like Monaghan, individuals who dream of being astronauts—a dream bespeaking our inner state of isolation.

Situating *The Falling Astronauts* in its historical, cultural, and literary milieu reveals a text that engages with the events current to its own age and dives headlong into a complex maelstrom of issues that informs our lives well after the (maybe not so) heroic deeds of the Apollo Program—a maelstrom bound to the pitfalls of the mediascape, the impact of technoscience on the human condition, the meaning or meaninglessness of individuals in the age of gigantic, worldwide organizations and systems, the tangled interface of sexuality in private and public sectors, the threat of nuclear annihilation, and the chasms and abysses of the collective unconscious. Reprinting this novel is an act of cultural recollection that may shed light on our own dark days.

Rome, Italy
2017

THE FALLING ASTRONAUTS

ABOUT THE AUTHOR

BARRY N. MALZBERG is an American writer, editor, and agent. His prolific career has spanned numerous genres, most notably crime and science fiction. Malzberg was particularly active in the SF scene of the early seventies, although he became disillusioned with the market forces defining the field and has rarely published SF works since. His most recent activity in the field has been in the form of advice columns for writers in the quarterly magazine of the Science Fiction and Fantasy Writers of America. Malzberg won the first John W. Campbell Memorial Award for *Beyond Apollo* in 1973. Over the years, his writing has been shortlisted for the Hugo, Nebula, and Philip K. Dick Awards, among others.

OTHER AOP TITLES

AN EARNEST BLACKNESS
Eugen Bacon

A SHORT, SHARP SHOCK
Kim Stanley Robinson

CITY PRIMEVAL
Robert Carrithers & Louis Armand

BEYOND APOLLO
Barry N. Malzberg

ENTROPOLOGY
Louis Armand

SPECTRE
Laurence A. Rickels

JACKANAPE & THE FINGERMEN
D. Harlan Wilson

NOSTALGIA
Hope Jennings

SHRAPNEL: CONTEMPLATIONS
Lance Olsen

SOFT INVASIONS
James Reich

TAO TE JINX: APHORISMS & QUOTATIONS
Steve Aylett

THE BLOT
Jonathan Lethem & Laurence A. Rickels

THE WAKE & THE MANUSCRIPT
Ansgar Allen